Copyright © 2014 by Cathie Pelletier
Cover and internal design © 2014 by Sourcebooks, Inc.
Cover design by Will Riley for Sourcebooks
Map design and illustration © Carl Hileman

Sourcebooks and the colophon are registered trademarks of Sourcebooks, Inc.

All rights reserved. No part of this book may be reproduced in any form or by
any electronic or mechanical means including information storage and retrieval
systems—except in the case of brief quotations embodied in critical articles or
reviews—without permission in writing from its publisher, Sourcebooks, Inc.

The characters and events portrayed in this book are fictitious or are used ficti-
tiously. Any similarity to real persons, living or dead, is purely coincidental and
not intended by the author.

Published by Sourcebooks Jabberwocky, an imprint of Sourcebooks, Inc.
P.O. Box 4410, Naperville, Illinois 60567-4410
(630) 961-3900
Fax: (630) 961-2168
www.jabberwockykids.com

Library of Congress Cataloging-in-Publication data is on file with the publisher.

Worzalla-USA, Stevens Point, WI
Date of Production: February 2014
Run Number: 5000581

Printed and bound in the United States of America.
WOZ 10 9 8 7 6 5 4 3 2 1

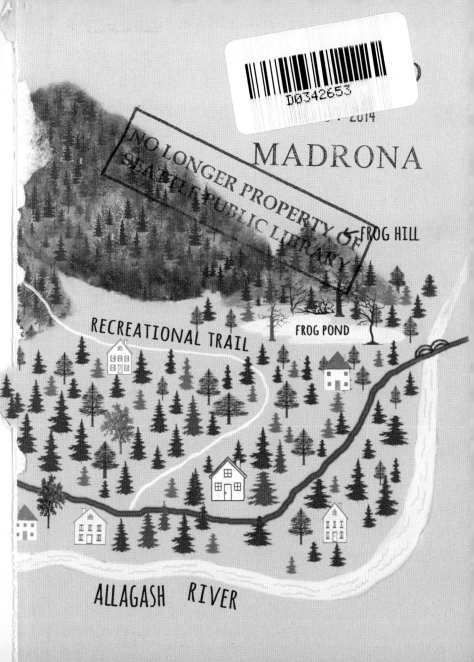

NO LONGER PROPERTY OF
SEATTLE PUBLIC LIBRARY

MADRONA

FROG HILL

RECREATIONAL TRAIL

FROG POND

ALLAGASH RIVER

The
Summer
Experiment

Cathie Pelletier

sourcebooks
jabberwocky

Doris Robichaud Lazore, *who always took part in my wild plans when we were kids growing up in Allagash, schemes which included running away from home (via the St. John River) on a raft built from my father's window shutters.*

Louis Allen Pelletier
& Ethel Tressa O'Leary Pelletier
for giving me the gift of childhood.

Contents

1
STRANGE LIGHTS

It was at Grandpa Carter's birthday party that we first saw the strange lights in the sky. Everyone but me, that is. Roberta Angela McKinnon. That's because I was in the kitchen getting a jar of mustard and my family was in the backyard. I don't like missing *anything*. Generally, I'm known to be at the heart of the action. Sometimes, I even cause it. But when I went back outside, everyone was staring up at the sky, mouths open, like a nest of baby birds waiting to be fed. I looked up and didn't see anything but stars.

"Holy cow!" said Uncle Horace.

"Wow!" Johnny said. "You missed it, Roberta!"

"What was it?" I asked. I handed the mustard to Grandpa so he could put it on his hot dog. Grandpa won't eat pasta. He says it's just not American. So Mom always cooks him a hot dog when we have Italian spaghetti or Chinese food.

"A weird light," Johnny said. "It moved really fast." Johnny is my big brother, and he is usually of sound mind. Usually. But now that he likes Miranda Casey, I'm doubtful.

"What did it look like?"

"It must have been some kind of jet," my dad said.

"I bet it's something new that the military is testing," said Uncle Horace. "Something secret."

"What color was it?" I asked.

"Maybe a weather balloon," said my mother. She was holding Tina, my baby sister, and looking at the mountain across the river. Tina is only four years old. I'm the middle kid, two years younger than Johnny, who is thirteen.

"Could it have been the International Space Station?" asked Aunt Betty.

"The space station doesn't move that fast," Uncle Horace said.

"How big was it?" I'd only been in the kitchen a minute. Surely they hadn't already forgotten that I existed.

"The Air Force is probably testing a new weapon," said Grandpa. He blames everything on Loring Air Force Base, even heavy snowfalls and summer lightning storms. And yet, the base has been closed for years.

"Will someone describe it to me, *please*?" I felt invisible.

"Maybe it was a helicopter from the forestry department," said Grandma. When Grandma has even one glass of wine, she can see all kinds of things. But everyone who was in the *backyard* had seen the light. Everyone who was in the *kitchen* hadn't.

"WHAT DID IT LOOK LIKE?"

They all stared at me like I was an alien or something. Mom and Dad say I tend to be dramatic. But it's not easy being the middle child. And then, it's not like excitement happens every day around here. Mostly, when school is out for the summer, I'm beyond bored. And God put me in the most perfect place for boredom to occur. I was born and raised in Allagash, Maine, right on the Canadian border. The middle kid in the middle of a wilderness. It's the land of trees and lakes at the very end of the road. No ocean. No department stores. No fancy restaurants. No cell phone reception. Even Stephen King lives way down in Bangor, five hours south. Allagash is probably too scary for Mr. King.

But for me, it's mostly boring. Now and then, tourists who come here to take the Allagash River trip claim to see lights in the sky. Since they're city people, they probably see moonlight bouncing off the horns of a moose and then panic. Rumors start that way. And we do have moose here. Plenty of them. Sometimes, I wake to see one swimming in the river behind my house or eating lettuce in my mom's garden. But it's a fact that tourists imagine all sorts of things once they get a few miles from an airport or a mall. Allagash tourists are a lot tougher than the city tourists who gather on the ocean down in southern Maine to eat lobster and sip wine. But they're still tourists. They come down the Allagash River all summer long in brightly colored canoes or kayaks. The blackflies bite them and the mosquitoes feed off them. But they seem to enjoy themselves, especially once they get back to their laptops.

So if any excitement happens, I'd like to be part of it.

"It was a big, white ball," said Dad. I finally got an answer. "And it had flashing lights on it."

"Where did it go?"

Johnny pointed across the river in the direction of Quebec, Canada.

"I hope those extraterrestrials got passports," said Uncle Horace, and grinned. Not many locals were happy when the law changed and now everyone needs a passport to go to Canada. Even if it's to have supper at the Maple Leaf Restaurant, which is just across the international bridge.

"I still think it was a weather balloon," Mom said. She was still holding my sister, her sweater wrapped around Tina's chubby little arms.

We all watched as Grandma lit the one huge candle in the middle of Grandpa's cake. On cue from Mom, we broke into a pretty bad version of "Happy Birthday to You." Grandma can hit notes so high that only dogs can hear them. This is why we own a cat.

"I can't believe that in four years I'll be seventy," said Grandpa when we finished.

"Good thing you didn't light sixty-six candles, Bob," my dad teased. "They'd probably see the glare all the way down in Bangor and think it's UFOs." Grandpa popped him a fake punch on his arm. He says my dad is his favorite son-in-law, but then, Dad is his *only* son-in-law.

"Roberta, would you go get Grandpa's present?" my mom asked. "It's in my bedroom."

Did I mention that the middle child is also the family slave? *Roberta, get this. Roberta get that.* Tina's too little and Johnny is too grown-up and self-important to fetch mustard and birthday presents. Sometimes, I wish aliens would take me. I really do. At least I'd be free.

I found the birthday present sitting on the end of my mother's bed. I slipped a finger in under the ribbon and lifted it. I let the screen door slam behind me as I stepped outside. I could see my family still gathered around the outdoor fireplace, all orange in the glow. Grandpa was telling them something funny, probably one of his stories about working at Loring Air Force Base before they closed it.

I started down the path, which is lined with my mom's lilac bushes. It's my least favorite place in the yard. At night, the bushes are spooky. They block the rays of porch light and cast shadows on the path. And that's when I did something very stupid. I remembered the

Allagash Abductions. Not all tourists who come here to take the river trip have a great time. One summer night in 1976, four men from Vermont put up their tents in a campground and then made a huge bonfire on the shore. They wanted it to burn for hours since it gets darker than dark in the woods at night. The four of them got in a canoe and paddled out into the lake to fish. That's when they saw a round, white ball in the sky. One of the guys signaled it with his flashlight. When it started coming toward the canoe, they paddled like heck. Next thing they know, they're onshore again and the big fire they had just made was almost out. Years later, they were hypnotized by an expert in UFOs. Sure enough, they'd been taken aboard a spaceship and examined by aliens, creatures with big heads and large black eyes. The man who hypnotized them wrote a book called *The Allagash Abductions*. So that's our claim to fame here in town. But don't take my word for this. Go ahead and google it. Go to YouTube.com and make up your own mind.

So there I was, standing in the shadows of Mom's lilac bushes right after my family had also seen a strange light in the sky. And now the bushes were moving in the wind like living things. *Bushes, for crying out loud, Roberta. Lilac bushes! Get a grip.* And that's when I saw it. It stepped out in front of me and stood there. The large, round head, the big, black eyes. I felt the birthday gift drop to the ground at my feet. My heart was beating so loudly that I could hear it. I tried to scream but nothing came out. "Help me, Mom! Save me, Dad!" Those words stayed in my mouth. And then the head, with those awful eyes, moved out of the shadows and right up to me. A round, white head with huge black eyes…

"*Mom!* Make Johnny stop scaring me!" Those words came out easily enough. And they got my mom's attention.

"Jonathan McKinnon, leave your sister alone and I mean this!" She always means it, but he never listens. Ever since he went to a movie with Miranda Casey, he thinks he's all that *and* a bag of chips. She may be the prettiest girl in school, but how smart can you be if you go to the movies with *my brother?*

"You are such a girl," Johnny whispered, laughing his mean laugh. Then he bounced the soccer ball he'd been holding in front of his face. Huge white head with big, black eyes? A soccer ball! "Good thing a sweater can't break or you'd be using your allowance to buy Grandpa a new gift."

I bent down and patted the ground near the lilac bushes, looking for the present. It had fallen on its side, but it seemed okay. And that's when it happened a second time.

"There it is again!" I heard my father say. "Now there are three of them!"

"Awesome!" said Johnny.

By the time I stood up, holding the present against my chest, it was over. Apparently the ball of light had zoomed back and brought a couple of friends. Or so I heard later from Mom. Then the lights disappeared over the mountain.

"Did anybody else hear a whirring sound?" Grandma wondered.

It took about thirty seconds for everyone to announce that they too had heard sounds, which varied somewhat. Humming. Buzzing. Droning. Whining. Purring. You name it and they'd heard it. Everyone but me.

I stood there staring up into the night sky. I could hear the fire snapping in the fireplace. I could hear frogs croaking down at Frog Pond in the meadow. I could hear June bugs hitting against the screen door, trying to get inside. I could hear Mr. Finley's dog barking from his doghouse a quarter mile down the road. I could hear the river lapping at rocks along the shore. But nothing whirred, hummed, buzzed, droned, whined, or purred. All I could see up in that enormous sky were thousands of softly twinkling stars. I could see the Milky Way streaking white across the heavens. And the crescent of moon, a fingernail above the mountain. I'd missed the excitement again.

That's when I felt something crawling, inching its slimy way along the back of my neck. I screamed as I whacked it away. It was a cold string of spaghetti held in the hand of my big brother.

"You are such a girl," he whispered. I didn't even bother to report this one to my mother. What good would it do? I was stuck until he got old enough to move out of the house. Before I went back to the picnic table for a big piece of birthday cake, which I most certainly deserved, I looked up into that heaven of stars.

"Take him, please," I whispered. "Abduct my brother. And don't ever bring him back."

2

FROG HILL

M ost people in the little town of Allagash didn't believe the story of the 1976 abductions. Some felt it wasn't good publicity for the town, that it might frighten away our tourists. Besides, there were worse things to worry about, such as if we could get a permit to use fireworks at the big Fourth of July celebration. That's why I was surprised the next day when everyone was talking about the strange lights.

At the post office, Lila Jandreau asked if I'd seen them.

"Nope," I said. I paid for the book of stamps my mom needed and then hurried out. I didn't want to hear how amazingly weird and altogether astonishing they were.

At the grocery store, Bill Flagg asked the same thing. Did you see those wild lights? Did you see how they zipped around and then just disappeared? *Did you see, did you see, did you see?* I was sick of being asked. Even old Mr. Finley, who has cataracts in both eyes, saw the lights. And so did his dog, Mutt, which is why I'd heard him barking last night.

The *Bangor Daily News* bragged about it: STRANGE LIGHTS SEEN OVER NORTHERN MAINE. HUNDREDS WITNESS THE SIGHTINGS. Well, count me out of the hundreds. Apparently, I'm doomed to suffer a life of boredom in the sticks at the end of the road. We don't even get any serial killers this far north. It's just too far for them to travel.

For the next week, it was like living in Crazy Town. There were all kinds of sightings by just about everyone. Mr. Cramer at the gas station. Faye Hafford at the library. Chad Putnam, who drives the UPS truck. Wayne McBridy, who manages Allagash Canoe Rentals. Darlene Dumond at the River Café. Vernon and Sylvia Martin, who own the tree farm. UFOs for sure, everyone said. Cigar-shaped, dish-shaped, ball-shaped, kidney-shaped, you name it.

However, the *Bangor Daily News* now quoted someone at an Air Force base in Vermont to put the mystery to rest.

"We have determined that the sightings in northern Maine over the past few days are caused by the reentry of rocket debris into Earth's atmosphere."

While most people didn't believe that, they *did* believe, like Grandpa, that the Air Force was up to no good. My dad and Uncle Horace agreed. Secret tests for planes or maybe helicopters. However, a few UFO fans such as Mrs. Cramer and Josh Turner were certain that aliens had visited Allagash again. To me, it didn't matter what the lights were. I just wanted to see them for myself. How else could I come to my own conclusions?

That's why I was happy to run into Sheriff Mallory at the post office. Sheriff Mallory is pretty wise and he sort of put things in place for me.

"Remember, Roberta," the sheriff said. "No matter what you see, hear, or read, everything has a logical explanation. Don't let folks fool you with all these sightings. I'm out there on patrol almost every night, and I've yet to see anything strange in the sky. I've seen the Space Station many times. Jupiter. Airplanes and shooting stars. It can all be explained."

That helped me a lot. But what finally brought me

peace was that my best friend, Marilee Evans, also didn't see anything extraterrestrial. Either that, or she was pretending so that I wouldn't feel so, well, *alienated*. Marilee and I have been best friends for almost a year, ever since her mom moved back home to Allagash after her divorce from Marilee's father. We bonded the first day we met, when I taught her how to pronounce *Allagash*. It's "Al-UH-gash," and not "ALL-uh-gash," with two "ls," the way some tourists say it.

"You could write a story for the school paper," said Marilee. "You know, how people have claimed to see UFOs for thousands of years. There are ancient caves around the world with drawings of spacecraft and creatures wearing helmets."

Marilee and I are about the smartest girls in our class. Well, not *about* the smartest, we truly are. I was just being modest. In science class, we're awesome. Our big dream is to win the Maine State Science Fair if we can just come up with an amazing project. And guess what? I'm blond! I don't know who started this "blonds are dumb" notion in the first place. Maybe a dark-haired boy like my brother, Johnny. I have long blond hair and I'm amazingly smart. You might say I'm narcissistic. But then, I can tell you without using Google who Narcissus was. I think this is why Johnny torments me. He calls me a science geek. But he's jealous since he has to work hard to get Cs when all I get are As. I can get an A with my eyes closed, which is what they were right then. Marilee and I were lying on the two gigantic rocks that we had claimed as our own on the bank of the river. They were almost the size of my bed and flat enough that we could stretch out while we found shapes in the clouds and discussed our boring lives.

"I guess I could write a story," I said. I was wearing my favorite T-shirt, which has Luke Skywalker's face just behind his X-wing starfighter. It belonged to my mom when she was a little girl. Johnny says I live in the past, but Luke Skywalker is eternal.

"By the way," said Marilee. "I think Henry is up to no good. I saw him yesterday sneaking into his mother's greenhouse, all secret-like."

This would be Henry Horton Harris Helmsby. A lot of the kids call him just Henry, but I secretly nicknamed him "the Four Hs of the Apocalypse." He is what is you

15

call a nemesis, an enemy that's tough to beat. *My* nemesis. Of the two science projects that I masterminded in the past, before Marilee moved to Allagash, I'd lost to "4 Hs" both times. That can lower your confidence and self-esteem. Even mine. But at least Henry lives next door to Marilee, which is good since she can keep an eye on him.

"We can outsmart Henry," I said. "But it won't be easy."

"He's such an egghead," Marilee said.

"Actually, Marilee, his head is shaped more like a cucumber than an egg." It was true. I figured Henry had such a big brain filling up the top of his head that he needed a lot of space below so that the brain could send down long roots. For brain nourishment, that is.

"He's up to something big all right," said Marilee. Just before school ended and Mrs. Dionne, our teacher, passed out forms for the science fair, Marilee and I decided to be partners, which is allowed. But HHHH is much too vain to let anyone be his partner, unless it was Luther Burbank or Gregor Mendel. Henry is a genius who always works alone. We needed to keep a close watch on him for sure.

"Let's start asking around," I said. "Quietly though, so Henry doesn't know we're on to him."

"You really think we can beat him?" Marilee asked.

"Sure we can," I said. "But we need a big project. Maybe we could interview those four men in Vermont by phone. You know, the ones who say they were abducted here in 1976." I figured that could be interesting. But I was still disappointed that I hadn't seen the strange lights for myself.

"Maybe," said Marilee, and the "maybe" trailed off as she said it. I could tell she was drifting to sleep, which she often does when we lie on our river rocks and talk. It's easy to fall asleep to the sound of the red-winged blackbirds that nest in the bushes nearby and the gentle lapping of the river against the bank.

"*Wake up!*" I shouted, and Marilee almost rolled off her rock. I can be dramatic at times, or so I've been told.

"What in the world?" she asked, rubbing her eyes.

"If the UFOs won't come to us," I said, "then we'll go to the UFOs."

"Explain this, please, before my brain explodes."

"We'll camp out," I said. "We can't go all the way to Eagle Lake where the Allagash Abductions took place. But we can pitch our tent on the hill behind Frog Pond. It's only a quarter mile from the house."

"But it's so spooky out there," said Marilee. "And froggy."

"All the better for a sighting," I said. "Come on, everyone knows UFOs never land in the middle of Times Square, or at the Super Bowl. It has to be spooky and… froggy."

"Still," said Marilee. "Honestly, Robbie, I don't really believe in them. My mom says it's all hogwash. And that the Air Force always has secrets. And that rocket debris really does burn as it falls back to earth. Why don't we rent a movie instead. What about *Cowboys and Aliens?*"

Marilee is taller than me, with dark brown hair that ends just below her ears. She's really cute and also smart, which I previously mentioned. But she's a big chicken. The Gutless Girl, I call her. The Spineless Wonder.

"Come on, Marilee," I begged. "We can bring a cooler of sodas and some sandwiches and chips and candy bars."

"Well," she said. "I guess I can ask my mom."

✳ ✳ ✳

So that's how two perfectly sane—and did I mention very intelligent?—girls, one with long blond hair and one with shorter brown hair, packed up junk food and sleeping bags and pillows and flashlights and went camping on the hill behind Frog Pond. It was just after we'd had our supper, or what Marilee calls "dinner" since she lived in Boston until her parents got divorced. My dad helped us load it all onto the back of his pickup truck. We jumped on too, just to keep stuff from flying off in the wind. And then, as Tina bounced on the seat beside him, Dad drove us through the meadow, which was a mass of red clover and yellow buttercups, all the way to Frog Hill.

"Remember now," he said, as he helped me unfold my two-person tent. "If you get scared, use your flashlights to walk home. That path can be tricky."

Kids are tough in the country. We spend a lot of time without our parents even knowing where we are. We're either four-wheeling on the mountain or fishing or picking berries. But I knew my dad was wondering if Marilee, having spent her first years in a big city like Boston, could handle a night on Frog Hill. That's why he and my mom refer to us as the country mouse and the city mouse.

"We'll be careful," I said, and winked at Dad. Marilee

didn't notice. She was unrolling our sleeping bags inside the tent.

"And if you meet any little green men," said Dad, "please don't bring them home. It'll upset the cat."

"They aren't green anymore, Dad," I said. "They look like large-eyed bugs."

"Please stop!" said Marilee. But she smiled, and I knew she was just pretending to be scared.

We watched as Dad's pickup truck bounced across the meadow and disappeared from sight.

"My mom isn't happy about this," said Marilee, "but she says if your parents think it's okay, it's probably okay." She wrapped a bandana around her hair to discourage blackflies, the scourge of the North Woods.

"Of course, it's okay," I said, and uncapped a bottle of soda pop. "Johnny and I have been camping up here alone since we were knee-high to a grasshopper."

"I hope there are no grasshoppers in the tent," said Marilee. Sometimes, she really is a city girl, but I've toughened her up a lot.

***

The sun was sinking. It was a soft June evening, and we sat outside the tent and talked our heads off about everything from school to our favorite books and movies. In many ways, when you're a kid in such isolated country, it's pretty much the same world our parents and grandparents grew up in. I mean, sure I sometimes wonder what it would be like to take the subway to school each day instead of riding my bike along a country road lined with daisies. Or what it would be like to walk down to a museum instead of to Cramer's Gas & Movie Rentals to rent a movie now that the Cramers have "gone Hollywood," as Grandpa puts it. But in other ways, it's the same world as in Los Angeles or Moscow because of the Internet. When you go on Facebook to talk to a new friend, you're just another kid on the planet Earth.

The sky was now a dark blue with pink fingers at the edges. All the frogs in the pond were talking back and forth. Stars were winking on. Just then I heard a twig snap, the way it does when someone or some*thing* steps on it.

"Did you hear that?" I asked Marilee. I felt her fingers clutch my arm.

"Who's there?" she asked, more a whisper than a

shout. The only reply belonged to a hoot owl that *hoo-hoo-hooted* from a distant perch.

"Must have been a deer," I said. "Or maybe a cone fell from a pine tree. Maine *is* the Pine Cone State, you know."

"But it sounded like *walking*," Marilee insisted.

"A deer walks," I said. "Haven't you noticed that it has four hooves?"

We waited a couple more minutes. When nothing else cracked or snapped or hooted, we went back to our talk. I knew it was just a matter of time until we got around to what boys we would date when our moms said we were old enough.

"I'd like to go on a date with Billy Ferguson one day," I said. Billy was a couple years older than me and Johnny's best friend. I had never confessed this to Marilee before. But it was a special night, and special nights are made for telling secrets.

"He's cute all right," said Marilee. "So is Johnny. See that?" She pointed up. "Shooting star."

I had seen it too, a silver thread disappearing in seconds beyond the mountain. But excuse me? My brother *cute*? Catch me as I pass out.

"Make a wish," I said. I watched as Marilee crossed her fingers and stared up at the sky where the star had just fallen. "Can I guess what you wished for?"

"Sure," she said, and smiled at me. I was so glad to have her as a friend. If it weren't for Marilee Evans, my boring life would be unbearable.

"That your mom and dad would get back together?" I asked. She knew I knew. We had talked about this many times in the months we'd been friends.

"I just wish he didn't live down in Boston," Marilee said. "I wish I could see him once a week, instead of every couple months."

"Hey," I said, changing the subject. I wanted this to be a fun night. "Let's play Guess the Famous Name until it's dark enough for aliens."

And so we did. I guessed all of Marilee's famous names. Marco Polo, Clara Barton, and Justin Bieber. And she guessed all of mine. Neil Armstrong, Nick Jonas of the Jonas Brothers, and President Lincoln. Sometimes, it can be boring to play a game with my best friend because we tend to think alike.

Marilee reached into the tent for her jacket. Overhead,

the stars were now sparkling and bright. I started counting them.

"Did you know that thousands of years ago, people thought the stars were little lanterns carried by the gods?" I asked.

"That's because they didn't have Bic lighters back then," said Marilee. She pointed to the southwest. "What's that? It's moving slowly this way." We both watched in silence until we saw red lights blinking under the wings of what was probably a jet airplane. I thought of all those passengers up there in the air, drinking coffee or eating pretzels or sleeping with their heads pressed against tiny airline pillows. It was a long way from gods carrying lanterns across the heavens. Suddenly, I saw weird lights bouncing on the pond. Up and down. Up and down. My heart froze.

"What's that?" Marilee asked.

"I'm not sure," I said. We sat for a few minutes, waiting, but the bouncing lights had disappeared. We could hear noises again in the woods, raccoons and skunks most likely. I prayed we wouldn't encounter a moose. But a country kid is used to sounds at night coming from the forest. That's the time a lot of wild animals forage for food.

"It had to be car lights from the main road," said Marilee.

"Maybe coming around that turn where Mr. Finley lives," I said. "There must be an open space in the trees."

Overhead, I could make out the summer constellations. The Great Square. Pegasus. Cassiopeia. There is nothing so awesome as sitting beneath the universe and peering up at it. That's something I wouldn't be able to do in a big city. Even if you could find a good spot, the light pollution would blind you. And that's what I was thinking when I heard a big splash in the pond. Marilee grabbed my arm again.

"Frog," I said. "It probably hopped off a log."

Marilee checked her watch. It was just after 10 p.m.

I was about to say, "Let's get some sleep," when I saw something shiny on the other side of the pond. It had to be more than five feet tall. Could it be the ruins of the brick chimney that had once been on the roof of Grandpa's cabin? The cabin had been gone for years but the old chimney stood in the brambles as a reminder. Then I remembered that Grandpa had toted the bricks away just that spring.

"Holy smokes," I heard Marilee say. "What is that,

Robbie?" Whatever it was, it was all lit up, from top to bottom. And it was not moving.

"I think it's a tree," I said, straining my eyes, wishing I had fox eyes right then.

"Why is a tree shining like that?" Marilee asked. That question had occurred to me too.

"I don't think it's a person," I said. I couldn't see a human head, and I couldn't tell if it even *had* feet. But soon we had the answers to our questions when the thing turned slowly in our direction. I saw the shape of a head then, and two arms. One leg stepped forward, silver as dimes in the beam of light that was hitting it. Then the other leg also took a step. Whatever this creature was, it was climbing Frog Hill to where our tent was pitched! I thought the scream I heard was mine until I realized it was Marilee's.

3
THE ALIEN

I t stood over five feet tall. I'd never seen anything so shiny. The face also seemed made of silver. I couldn't see any eyes, but that didn't matter. It was definitely climbing the hill. I wanted to die. I wanted to sink into the earth. As I scrambled to my feet, all I could think of was Marilee. This was *my* idea. She could have been home with her mother right then, safe and sound. She was my best friend and I'd put her in danger. I reached inside the tent and grabbed my flashlight. Then I grabbed Marilee's hand. To heck with our sleeping bags and the tent. We could come back tomorrow for our stuff, when the sun was shining bright.

"We need to run!" I whispered. But where? The only path up the hillside, about two hundred feet long, was the very one this creature was climbing. We'd have to escape down the hill behind us, which meant blackberry brambles and burdocks and hobble bushes that could trip us. Down we went, the arms of our jackets pulled at and torn by brambles, our feet stepping in holes, our hands trying to balance each other. The flashlight lit our way but once I even dropped it. It was like plowing through a black jungle. But knowing what was climbing Frog Hill kept us going.

Finally, we reached the bottom. Shaken, we stumbled out onto the main road near Old Man Finley's house. I heard Mutt send out a volley of sharp barks.

"We'd better get out of here before Mr. Finley shoots at us," I said to Marilee. He was known to take his shotgun down if a breeze rattled the leaves in his yard.

We made our way along the road, the beam of the flashlight bouncing in front of us. And then, as we rounded the curve where the old pine grows, I saw the lights of my house up ahead. I silently said my usual "Thank you, God" prayer, in which I promise I'll never do anything stupid again. I've said that prayer lots of times.

"Let's sit on the swing," I said. "Catch our breath before we go inside."

The swing is on our lawn, below the house, and it would be private. Marilee hadn't said much the whole time, and I knew she was just too scared to talk. What had I called her? Big Chicken. The Gutless Girl. Spineless Wonder. Well, I was all of those things and more. I could see my mother inside the kitchen, doing the dishes. It was such a warm and safe picture. Dad was sitting in front of the television set, its screen flickering on the frames of his glasses.

"Did we just see what I think we saw?" Marilee finally asked after we had swung silently for a minute, back and forth, back and forth. "What *was* that?"

"An extraterrestrial, what else?" I said. "I believe in them now. I can tell you that much."

"Did you see its face?"

"No. Did you?"

Marilee shook her head.

"I don't think it had a face," she said. "I think it was all silver." She bit at her fingernail, which is what she always does when she is nervous beyond belief. "Who do we tell? Your mom and dad? My mom? Mr. Purdy the principal? Sheriff Mallory? No one?"

"No one," I said, and I meant it. "We'll just get laughed at." Besides, I knew by heart what everyone would say. What had Sheriff Mallory told me? *No matter what you see, hear, or read, everything has a logical explanation.* Well, this didn't.

"But what if we're in danger?" she asked. "What if the whole town is in danger? Those things can't just go walking around in the night. What does it want?"

I didn't know. This was bigger than a test question. Ask me who Pierre and Marie Curie are, and I can tell you. Ask me what was climbing Frog Hill and I'm gonna flunk. That's when we heard the bikes pedaling down the tarred road that ran in front of our house. At first, I felt the fear again until I thought, "They have superfast spaceships. They fly through wormholes. They don't ride bikes." And then I heard talking. Human voices. It sounded like my brother, Johnny. But he had gone to Billy Ferguson's house for the night. Then I heard Billy's voice too.

"Shhh," I said to Marilee. We were sitting in darkness on the swing. No one would see us. The bikes cranked into the yard. We watched from the shadows as Johnny and Billy jumped off and kicked their stands down. They seemed to be having a great time.

"Did you see them run?" Johnny asked. "I was laughing so hard I almost tore the aluminum foil."

"I can't believe they fell for it," said Billy. "If they hadn't run, if they'd let you get closer, they could have seen how stupid you looked. All that foil and Scotch tape!"

Oh my God. Billy Ferguson!

It had just hit me. Had they sneaked up there early enough to hear the talk Marilee and I shared? I remembered the noise earlier of a twig snapping and Marilee's comment that it sounded like someone walking. I know she was thinking the same thing because I saw the silhouette of her head as she turned and looked at me. I squeezed her hand as if to say, "Oh, I hope they didn't hear!"

"I should have let *you* be the alien," Johnny was saying now. He was pulling wads of aluminum foil out of his backpack. And other junk. Probably the Scotch tape. And the flashlight that Billy obviously had shone on my brother, lighting him up for all the frogs to see. The frogs and the Spineless Wonders. "She wouldn't have run if it had been *you*, Billy."

And then, he imitated my voice, making it squeaky as he always does when he mocks me. "I think I'd like to go on a date with Billy Ferguson one day." I heard them laugh. Johnny *and* Billy Ferguson. I died a thousand deaths in that minute. A million deaths. I felt Marilee's arm wrap around my shoulders to comfort me. It was her way of saying, "Listen, best friend, this will pass. Don't be ashamed for the rest of your life and then some."

When they had stored the stuff under the front porch, where Johnny would most likely find and destroy it tomorrow, they kicked up the stands on their bikes. I watched as they pedaled away into the night, back to Billy's house most likely. I imagined they would tell the tale over and over until dawn, until they couldn't laugh anymore. Who else would they tell? The other kids when school started again in the fall? Maybe they would call up *Good Morning America* so the whole country could be in on the joke.

"It was nothing but mean," Marilee said, now that the bikes were just creaking noises in the night. "They'll be paid back for this one day. You watch and see, Roberta."

I stepped off the swing. We would tell no one what

happened. We would pretend it had been a great night on Frog Hill looking at the stars. We came home because we were cold. *Tell no one*, for that's what Johnny would want. I imagined him grinning his toothy grin as we told Mom and Dad about the silver-colored alien.

"Johnny is gonna pay for this, all right," I said. My voice was no longer shaking. In the place of fear was anger. Anger mixed with shame. *I think I'd like to go on a date with Billy Ferguson one day*. "This is now a declared war. And it's gonna be deadly."

4
EARTHLY REVENGE

With the sun shining in my window the next morning, I could think of nothing but revenge. I didn't care if Mom and Dad grounded me for life. If what happened last night got around school, my life was over anyway. I thought of moving to a cabin in the middle of the Allagash wilderness where no one would ever find me. But what good was that? Besides, my brother would win that way. And I was determined that he lose the next battle and, therefore, the war.

"Roberta!" Mom's voice, loud and clear at the bottom of the stairs. "Marilee's mother is on the phone."

I reached over and shook Marilee awake.

"Your mom wants to talk to you," I said. I reached for the cordless phone in my bedroom, clicked it on, and said, "Hey, Catherine." That's what Marilee's mother said I should call her, by her first name. I guess things are different in Boston than they are in Allagash. I handed the phone to Marilee. I left her talking to her mom, telling her how much fun we had last night. I closed the door behind me and went down the hallway to Johnny's bedroom. I cracked open the door and saw that his bed was still made. So he had spent the night at Billy's after all. Good. I hope they had an awesome time, a memorable night. I sat down at his laptop, which was still open on his desk. I flicked it on and waited as it whirred to life, a little spaceship of its own. When I had his e-mail account pulled up, I searched until I found the e-mail address for Miranda Casey: MirCase@mail.com.

So how mean is too mean? What's the limit? I wanted to be mean, no doubt about it, since that's what Johnny had been. But I had more good in my bones than Johnny did. You'd think we were raised in totally separate families. Mom keeps saying my brother is going through a rough period. "Adolescence is tough for young boys," she says. "He'll grow out of it and you two will be great friends one day." Right.

Maybe in a galaxy far, far away. But not on Earth. Not in my lifetime. I just couldn't see it. Mom said that the day I gazed up at my beloved *Star Wars* poster, pinned to my bedroom wall, and was shocked to see that Princess Leia had two front teeth missing. There were just black spaces where those beautiful white teeth should have been. She also had a thick, black mustache and two bushy, black eyebrows, which made her look like Chewbacca's little sister. But at least my mom made Johnny buy me a new poster.

I copied Miranda's address in a new e-mail and then sent it to myself. I had to have more time to think about this. *How mean is too mean?* I knew all about those kids who were so terrible on Facebook that some teenagers even changed schools just to get away from them. Big, cruel bullies. And adults did it too. There was no way I could be that mean. I wanted to be kind of lukewarm mean. Now that I had the e-mail address I needed, I would plan carefully.

In the kitchen, Mom had pancakes waiting for us in a dish on the stove. There was a note propped up against the cookie jar.

Tina and I gone shopping. Fresh fruit and orange juice in refrigerator.

Love, Mom

I brought the pancakes over to the table. Marilee was just pulling out a chair.

"Last night sucked," I finally said, since we weren't talking. We were reliving the horror instead. The silvery creature. The scary run down a hillside with no path. If I told on Johnny, I think this trick would really get my parents' attention. They'd punish him good. I could hear my dad's voice now. "Do you realize your sister and Marilee could have broken a leg or even worse? You need a serious readjustment, buddy."

But if that happened, I couldn't put my payback plan in motion. All I'd get would be a few days of satisfaction in knowing that Johnny wasn't allowed to go on the Internet for a week or watch his favorite sports shows. I was thinking far bigger than *that*.

"You're up to something," said Marilee, and I remembered that we were having breakfast together. "I have a hunch it's not about the science fair and Henry Helmsby's project."

"Sorry," I said, "but you're right. My mind is working on revenge, not science. And it's gonna be priceless."

"I have to go," said Marilee. She seemed upset, and I knew it wasn't just about last night.

"Something wrong I don't know about?" I asked. I could always read her like a bestselling book.

"My mom says she heard from Dad this morning. He's getting married next month."

I watched out the kitchen window until Marilee's bike disappeared down the road.

★ ★ ★

First, I rode my four-wheeler out to Frog Hill to pack up our tent and sleeping bags. Then, sleep deprived as I was, thanks to my evil brother, I went out to the swing with a pillow and a notepad. I positioned the pillow behind my back as I began to scribble ideas. So how mean *is* lukewarm mean? I probably couldn't use Super Glue or a staple gun. Mom and Dad would really freak out. But

I wanted to scare Johnny even more than he had scared me. How? That was my dilemma as I pushed the swing into motion. It was warm and sunny in the yard. I could hear the buzz of bumblebees as they visited Mom's flower garden. I wondered if other galaxies would have flowers. Or maybe there is a planet of giant orange poppies and all the aliens look like bumblebees! I yawned once or twice before I let the notepad fall into my lap.

I am running. There are beings chasing me. I can't see them well in the moonlight, but they have big eyes in big bug-like heads and I am terrified. One reaches out a tentacle and wraps it around my wrist. He is wearing a white jacket and he seems to be the leader. I feel my insides heave up. I am trying to tell this creature, this insect, to let go of me. But it is holding me tight, another tentacle now circling my other wrist.

And now I see more insects, bug-like things with bug-like hands. They are standing outside a spaceship that looks like a loaf of French bread, long and narrow. I'm screaming and screaming, and now the head insect—maybe he's a doctor on their planet or something like that?—leans down close to my face. He looks just like a bumblebee! He isn't saying the words but I can hear them. I can pick up his thoughts, his brain sending them to my brain. I'm horrified. I can't move an inch. But Dr. Bumblebee is telling me not to be afraid.

"Wake up, idiot!"

Excuse me? What did that big bumblebee just say, or think, to me?

"Wake up, Robbie."

How does this alien insect know my name? Now Dr. Bumblebee is shaking me hard.

"Please don't!" I shout. "Don't touch me, Dr. Bumblebee! I want to go home!"

"WAKE UP!"

I opened my eyes, squinting at the bright sunshine, and there was Johnny, leaning down over me in the porch swing. He had his hands on my shoulders. Why was my brother shaking me? He should be protecting me instead.

"Save me, Johnny." I mumbled the words.

"You're dreaming," Johnny said. "You are such a girl!"

Now I opened my eyes really wide and looked around. I was in the swing in our yard, right where I had fallen asleep. So I dreamed that whole thing? That's what I get for watching the Allagash Abductions on YouTube. It was an old episode of *Unsolved Mysteries*. I wondered which was scarier, Dr. Bumblebee or Johnny's stupid face. But there it was, looming in front of me, with his stupid grin and that tiny gap between his front teeth.

When I want to be mean back, I say, "Dude, what's that gap in your teeth? A parking space for a brown M&M?" That always gets to him. So that's what I said.

"Hey, Indiana Jones," he said, ignoring my insult. "Shouldn't you be in Roswell looking for spaceships? What are you doing sleeping in the middle of the day?"

I said nothing. I grabbed my pillow and my notepad where I had even drawn some alien faces with big bug eyes. But, mostly, I had made some important notes for my Plan of Revenge. I stomped off to my room.

"Be patient," I told myself as I slammed my door. "Victory will soon be yours and it will be oh so perfect."

In my room, I sat at my computer and typed the words I'd scribbled on my notepad. I read them again carefully to be sure they were correct. I can't help myself. This is why I get all As in school. I always check spelling, grammar, neatness, food spills, cat paw prints, you name it.

Dear Miranda,

Please meet me TONIGHT after dark at the picnic table on Peterson's Mountain, near Calley's Creek. PLEASE do not tell anyone or it will spoil my plans! I have something IMPORTANT to tell you. Tonight's the night! Keep this secret, okay? I know I can trust you.

Always, Johnny.

I figured Miranda had to know Peterson's Mountain. Everyone in town knows that mountain well. But I couldn't take any chances. I attached the crude map I had drawn up, simple enough that a Neanderthal could find Calley's Creek and the picnic table. I marked the e-mail "To Send Later." I wasn't ready yet. I had lots of things to do in order to prepare. Just as my brother prepared when he bought all that aluminum foil and tape.

Back in the kitchen, my mom was just hanging up the telephone. She turned to look at me.

"That was Grandma," she said. "This sounds

unbelievable, but Sheriff Mallory is calling a press conference this afternoon with the local TV station. Apparently,
he saw a UFO last night and he wants to talk about it."

5
A Close Encounter

Y ou folks have known me a lot of years," said Sheriff Mallory. He was staring into the TV cameras like that deer you hear about, the one that's gazing into the headlights. "I always try to be upfront and truthful." He paused, nervous. He pulled at the top button of his shirt collar, as if it might be choking him.

"He's never been good in front of the camera," my grandma whispered. "We were in the same graduating class. In 1965. Stanley Mallory was the valedictorian, but he was too shy to give the address. So we didn't have one that year. He's as honest as the day is long."

We were all sitting in our living room. The whole gang had gathered for this press conference. My mom and dad. Grandma and Grandpa. Uncle Horace, who is Mom's only brother, and his wife, Aunt Betty. Johnny the Menace. Marilee's mother had come over to watch with us. She was sitting next to Marilee on the sofa. Even Baby Tina was there, lying on her stomach on the floor, coloring some picture in a book.

"So I have to tell you the truth," Sheriff Mallory was saying now, "about what I saw last night on Highway 42, about a mile from where you turn off to Tom Leonard's farm. My job is to protect this town. And that's why I called this press conference. Last night, I saw a genuine UFO."

A lot of reporters had turned up. They all began to shout questions at once. It looked like a big-city story and we were all pretty impressed.

"Did you see actual beings?" one reporter yelled. He had a little plastic card pinned to his shirt that said PRESS.

"Were you taken aboard the spacecraft?" yelled another.

"What did the craft itself look like?" shouted a woman in a crisp red suit.

Sheriff Mallory held up his hand, asking for order.

"Poor Stanley," said Grandma. "He's never been camera-friendly."

"No, I didn't see any beings and I wasn't taken aboard the craft," said the sheriff. "Please be patient and let me tell you what happened. It was just before midnight. I had driven out to Tom Leonard's farm. As some of you folks know, Tom is visiting his daughter in Florida for a couple weeks. He asked me to keep an eye on the place while he's gone. So I've been driving out there each night before I go off duty. Last night, on my way back from the farm, I noticed a light out my passenger window. What I saw was a large, triangular craft with a lot of white lights circling it. It was flying about fifty feet above the ground and traveling at the same speed I was, which was about forty-five miles an hour."

"That's not very fast for a spaceship," a reporter commented.

"I understand that," said Sheriff Mallory. He pulled a white handkerchief from his pocket and wiped sweat from the back of his neck. "That's why I was under the impression it was following me."

"Did you stop your car?" Someone I couldn't see, at the back of the room, shouted that question.

Sheriff Mallory shook his head.

"No, I didn't think that would do any good. I felt I was in danger enough as it was. I gotta tell you, folks.

It's a hair-raising experience to be out on that farm road alone and see something like that."

Grandma passed a bowl of popcorn she'd made over to my reaching hand. I saw Johnny staring at the television set, his face all concerned. So aliens weren't so funny now, were they? Marilee also saw, so she and I exchanged a quick smile.

"I don't believe I've ever seen Stanley so worked up," Grandma said. "Not even when Allagash lost the big basketball game to Fort Kent and, therefore, the 1964 tournament. He was our captain."

"Was there any noise, Sheriff?" This question came from Andrew Birden of *Fiddlehead Focus* in nearby Fort Kent. I recognized him because he visited our class on Career Day to talk to us about becoming journalists. I happen to think I'd make a good one.

"The craft made no noise whatsoever," said the sheriff.

"When did it disappear?" This question was again from the red-suited woman. She wore lipstick to match her outfit.

"It followed me for about two minutes, all the way down Highway 42. Then the lights on the craft began to glow brightly. As I watched, it rose slowly into the air and hovered at about three hundred feet. I saw just how huge the thing was. It had to be twice the size of a football field. Then it banked to the left over Paul Ellory's dairy farm. And when it did, the entire area below was lit up just like it was day. I could see Paul's cows and his red tractor and his two silos. I tell you, I've never witnessed anything like it before in my life."

"Could it have been an Air Force craft?" asked a man in a blue sweater. He was scribbling furiously on a yellow legal pad.

"I suppose it could," said Sheriff Mallory. "And I suppose it could have been a pig that learned to fly."

"Ha-ha!" Grandma said, and slapped her knee. "Stan is terrible with cameras, but he's got a sense of humor that won't quit!"

"I wish you'd stop talking about him," said Grandpa.

"Now, now," Grandma said. "I only dated Stan a couple times. There's no need for you to be jealous."

"Quiet!" said my mom, and cranked up the volume on the TV. Someone in the front row had his hand up to ask a question.

"Oh, that's crazy Joey Wallace!" said Mom. "Twenty-five years old and going on ten. He'll ask something foolish for sure. He's such a showoff."

"Sheriff, I know you like a beer or two to relax," Joey was saying, all smiling and pleased with himself. "Any chance you had a six-pack in the car?"

I saw smiles on the faces in the room. Some of the reporters lowered their heads so Sheriff Mallory wouldn't see them laughing at Joey's question.

"Shame on you, Joey," said Grandma. "What an insult to a fine man."

"I thought you only dated Stan once," said Grandpa.

"Quiet, everyone!" said my dad.

Sheriff Stanley Mallory put his hat back on and straightened his tie. He looked Joey Wallace right in the face.

"I won't dignify that question with an answer," he said. "This press conference is over."

★ ★ ★

Mom turned off the television but everyone stayed to talk about what had just happened. Dad and Grandpa and

Uncle Horace still believed that with Loring Air Force Base closed, this was the perfect place for secret testing by other bases.

"When planes leave the Air National Guard Base in Burlington, Vermont," my dad said, "they fly northward, right over the Allagash wilderness."

I figured he had a good point. Since we're so isolated here, well, better a few people seeing strange lights than everyone in New York City.

"And remember," said Uncle Horace, "it wasn't too many years ago that the Flying Wing would have scared the religion out of us. That's one weird-looking craft."

"That's true," said Grandpa. "They've been experimenting with tailless planes since the Wright brothers. And there are helicopters out there now that don't even look like helicopters."

"What about that delta wing someone over in England made out of metal?" asked Uncle Horace. "Even aliens would be afraid to ride on that thing."

Sometimes, it's fun to ask the adults a few questions you know they can't answer. This may be the reason I was born.

"Didn't Sheriff Mallory say it was twice the size of a

football field? Are helicopters that big? Do big airplanes fly that close to the ground?"

No one spoke for a few seconds.

"Darn Air Force," Grandpa finally said.

"If Stan Mallory says he saw a UFO," Grandma was saying as Marilee and I sneaked out of the room, "then he saw a UFO."

*** ***

We stood on the back porch steps and thought about what had just happened. Sheriff Mallory was as respected as could be in Allagash. I was so impressed that I put my plan for revenge on a back burner.

"You know what this means, don't you?" I asked, and Marilee nodded. "It means aliens are really out there, and they're visiting this area again. So our chances of contacting them just got better."

"Well, we'll need better chances," said Marilee. "I finally found out what Henry Helmsby is doing for his science project. He's crossing a Maine potato with a red turnip. I think we should be worried."

"Are you kidding?" I asked. "What's to worry about?" I was *very* worried. Henry adores Gregor Mendel, that monk who first discovered that plants have genes and peas taste good if you put butter on them. Okay, I made up that last part, but you know who I mean.

"He's calling it the Helmsby Poturn," she added. "You've got to admit that Henry is brilliant."

"Sure, but so is Venus. When was the last time Venus won anything?"

"Silly," said Marilee, grinning. "Venus is a planet."

"So is Henry Helmsby," I said. "At least, he moves in a different orbit than earthlings do." It was true. Brains and common sense don't always march hand in hand.

"I hope you're right," said Marilee. "He gives me the creeps. Every night I can see him from my bedroom window. He even wears a lab coat and goggles when he goes out to his mom's greenhouse. How weird is that?"

"Honestly, I can't see his project winning," I said, wanting to reassure her. "I mean, who is going to walk into the River Café and say to Darlene, 'Give me the mashed *poturns* and gravy, with meatloaf and a side of corn?' Who is going to play with a toy called

Mr. *Poturn* Head? Is Joey Wallace a couch *potato* or a couch *poturn*?"

"But the judges are all science geeks," said Marilee. "They don't even know about Mr. Potato Head."

"Well then, think of this fact," I pushed on. "What girl in the county will be excited to be crowned Miss Maine Poturn Blossom Queen at the state fair?" I think that last one hit home. I mean, even the science geeks turn out every potato harvest to watch the queen ride by in Sherry Sullivan's pink Cadillac convertible, the one she got by selling the most cosmetics in New England.

"You're right," Marilee said. "I never thought of it that way. Aliens are a lot more exciting than potatoes and turnips anyway."

I should be a lawyer. I really should.

6
The Setup

And then I quickly brought my plan for revenge back to the front burner. Before the press conference, I had asked my mom about Marilee and me using the four-wheelers, hers and Dad's. As I said, this is timber country. Huge trucks loaded with logs and headed to the paper mills are a daily sight on our highways. My dad, and just about every man in town, works for the P. G. Irvine Lumber Company, the biggest one in Maine. Dad operates heavy logging equipment such as a de-limber and a skidder. We're also in pickup-truck heaven since that's the most practical vehicle for this place. The roads have a lot of potholes due to wear from the big trucks driving over them. And they also have frost heaves, those mounds that push up under the tarred surface, thanks to our strenuous winters.

We're also known for snowmobiles in the winters and four-wheelers in the summers. Just about every family in town has a four-wheeler or two. Mom and Dad are members of a club so our family owns two. I taught Marilee how to drive one shortly after she moved to town, and now she handles it as well as any other country kid. The machines are used mostly for recreation. But on this day, I needed the family four-wheelers for business, not pleasure. And with everyone still arguing over what Sheriff Mallory saw, and with Grandma still making Grandpa jealous, we were free to fly.

"Wear helmets!" Mom yelled out the window when she heard me start up Dad's machine. I hate a helmet, but I'm no fool. My head is just another watermelon if it hits the tarred road at thirty miles an hour. With Marilee on Mom's smaller machine and pulling up the rear, we roared out of my driveway and headed across the meadow. Instead of turning toward Frog Pond, we kept going past the hill where we'd run down through blackberry brambles the night before. From there, we hit one of the recreation trails and stayed on it until we reached Peterson's Mountain. Driving the four-wheelers there is legal so long as we stay off the main highways.

Peterson's Mountain was owned by Marcus Peterson in the 1890s. Therefore, he was dead and gone long before I was born. Just his name is left as a reminder that he once walked among us. But there's a family graveyard up on the mountain. All the Petersons were buried there since they lived in isolation back then, as did a lot of old-timers. The graveyard is believed to be haunted since, well, it's very old and there are even graves for babies and young children. Four generations of Petersons were born, raised, and died up on that mountain. It's a place we Allagashers often use to test each other. "You think you're so brave? How about spending a night all alone on Peterson's Mountain?"

The only proof now of those families that once lived up there, other than their names on weathered, vine-covered stones, are the remains of a few old foundations and water wells, sunken into the earth and forgotten. It's a creepy place. I mean, there are even stones, just plain rocks, for two dead dogs in that graveyard. What's scarier than a ghost dog? Nothing, unless it's a ghost baby, one that cries in the woods just as the clock strikes midnight. But as scary as the place is in the middle of a sunny day, I never once saw anything unearthly there. Not yet, anyway.

However, come 7 p.m., the sun would be sinking and casting shadows this way and that. All those pines and spruce would be blocking the dying sunlight and catching up moonlight instead. Was there any better place for my plan?

Meet me TONIGHT after dark at the picnic table on Peterson's Mountain, near Calley's Creek.

I knew that if a pretty girl sent Johnny a note to meet her on *Mars,* he'd show up five minutes early. But I wondered if Miranda Casey would be too afraid to come. She spent a lot of time in the girls' bathroom at school, staring at her face in the mirror. Or fluffing up her already fluffy hair. I guess it would all depend on how crazy she was over my stupid brother.

Oh, did I tell you that Calley's Creek was named after Mr. Peterson's twelve-year-old daughter, Calley? It happened a hundred years ago, back at the turn of the century in 1914. Calley caught pneumonia. In her delirium, she left her sickbed late one night and wandered out into a raging snowstorm. The next morning, Old Man Peterson found her lying next to the icy creek, still dressed in her white nightgown. She had frozen to death. Southern Maine might be known for its big fancy ocean, its seafood, and its crimson sunsets. But up here we're known for blackflies, moose, and raging snowstorms. It was just Calley's bad luck not to have lived in Portland. If she had, she might have wandered down to the ocean and ordered a lobster.

Where you're born can affect your entire life.

Everyone in town has heard of Calley's Creek and the sad story of how she died. It's said she still walks those woods at night, following the creek back upstream and trying to find her way home.

Meet me TONIGHT after dark at the picnic table on Peterson's Mountain, near Calley's Creek.

Are you picturing this as I am? Who needs aliens to scare the daylights out of someone when a ghost story is right in my own backyard?

This trip on the four-wheelers up to Peterson's Mountain was, however, a test run. As I said, I'm a perfectionist. I get things done right. And if you're going to scare the daylights out of someone, it has to happen at night. I'd need this evening to prepare. Then tomorrow, once the sun had set, the real deal could go down. So, up we drove to the top of Peterson's Mountain.

Marilee pulled up beside me when we reached the picnic table that the Chamber of Commerce had put there for visitors. From that high spot, early evening, you can see all the lights of town twinkling like fireflies down below. At times like that, if I was with Mom and Dad, I always got a safe feeling, sort of like peering down on our own lives. You can forget about ghost dogs and frozen dead girls and just concentrate on how lucky you are to be alive. And to have both parents there to raise you. I knew Marilee was hurting over the news that her dad was going to marry his girlfriend. That ended the dream that her parents would get back together one day.

I turned off the four-wheeler and removed my helmet. Marilee did the same. We sat for a few seconds, not speaking, just looking down at the town of Allagash. Pickups and logging trucks and cars darted back and forth like important bugs.

"It's pretty, isn't it?" I didn't really mean it as a question since I've always loved the view. But Marilee was squea-mish, being that city mouse at heart.

"Pretty freaky," she said. "Where did that girl die?"

"Calley Peterson? Right there where you're sitting," I said, and smiled when I saw her jump. But then I remembered how scared I'd been on Frog Hill. "The creek runs down the mountain over there," I said, and pointed. "The old foundations for the buildings and the family graveyard are on the other side. Over there." I nodded at the west side of the mountain.

"Robbie, I don't know if I can go through with this," Marilee said. "I mean, it's still daylight and it's already a scary place. After sunset, it'll be a horror movie. Look, I've got goose bumps."

"Now you begin to realize my genius," I said.

"And what about Sheriff Mallory's press conference?"

"You heard my dad and uncle and Grandpa," I said, reassuring her. "Flying wing. Metal delta wing. Weird-looking helicopters. Even honest people like Sheriff Mallory make mistakes. Don't be afraid, Marilee. I'll be with you."

"That's another reason I've got goose bumps."

"Come on," I said. "I want to be sure of the light so I don't trip and break my neck. Otherwise, in a hundred years, they'll be calling this place Roberta's Creek."

I got off the four-wheeler and walked a few feet from the path. To the left of the picnic table was a large pile of brush, as high as my head. It was probably put there by park rangers who were cleaning the area.

"There's the perfect place for me to hide," I said. "I'll already have Mom's white nightgown over my clothes. All you have to do is turn on the light."

The light I chose for this mission was another sign of genius. It was Dad's night fishing lamp, a lantern-shaped thing that gives off a bluish light, an eerie glow. "Otherworldly" is the adjective that comes to mind. And that's the word I'll use when I write about my prank for the school paper this coming autumn. That is, unless Brother Johnny agrees to keep his big mouth shut about how scared I was on Frog Hill. And even more than that, what I said about wanting to date Billy Ferguson one day. I believe this is called blackmail.

"Can't we leave now?" Marilee asked. "It's bad enough I have to come up here tomorrow night."

I looked at my watch. Six thirty. The sun would set around seven.

"Not much longer," I said. "Come look. There's my house."

Marilee got off the four-wheeler and put her helmet on the seat.

"I've only seen it a dozen times," she said.

"There's your house too. See?" I pointed to the yellow house that sat on Main Street, at the edge of town near Cramer's Gas & Movie Rentals.

"I wonder if Mom is home yet," Marilee said. "I wonder if she's talking on the phone to Hank Preston, her new boyfriend. If your parents decide to date or marry someone new, shouldn't their kid get to choose who it is?"

"I'm sorry, Marilee," I said. "Life sucks sometimes."

"I know," she nodded. "Do you think if I ran away, maybe downstate somewhere, that Mom and Dad would get back together? You know, join forces so they can find me."

"I don't know," I said. But what I really thought was, "I doubt it." I shooed away the mosquito that had found my neck and was probably informing a zillion other

63

mosquitoes that fresh meat was in the woods. We'd need to bring fly repellent tomorrow night, what the locals call "fly dope." That, or be slowly cannibalized.

"God, what if *she* got involved in the hunt?" Marilee said then. "What if she and my dad bonded even more as he searched for me?"

"What's her name?" I asked.

"Dad calls her Sarah," Marilee said. "But I call her *she*."

The sun had set and a gray hue covered the mountain. Below us, the firefly lights of town were winking. It would be a dark ride down the narrow mountain path, a trail lined with the thick branches of pines and spruce. But we had our faithful four-wheelers with their yellow headlights. I went over to the brush pile and crouched behind it.

"Can you see me?" I asked.

"No," I heard Marilee say.

"Okay, here's where you can hide to shine the light on me." I pointed to a fat pine tree that grew ten feet from the brush pile. Marilee came and stood behind the pine.

"So I hold the lamp about this high and point it at you?"

"That looks about right," I said. I wished now I'd

brought the lamp with us for the test run. Dumb. But it would work. I could see it so clearly in my mind. Me standing up suddenly from behind the brush, dressed in deathly white, being lit up by a ghostly blue light. Should I moan as I stuck both arms out straight? Or just begin walking toward them?

Johnny would probably arrive first, being Johnny and so infatuated with Miranda. His four-wheeler would purr up the mountain, or Dad's four-wheeler rather. Then Miranda would arrive, probably on her brother's machine since I'd seen her riding it often with her friends. They would meet at the picnic table and she'd ask, "What did you want to tell me?" But before it could go any further, I'd stand up in my death gown and Marilee would blast me with blue light. Calley Peterson, trying to find her way home.

I should be given an Oscar.

"Let's go," I said. "Plan Roberta is in cement."

We started our machines and flicked on our head-lights. Helmets on, we circled around the picnic table and headed down the mountain, Marilee in the lead. I slowed for the sharp turn halfway down since I'd almost run over a rabbit there once. I figured it was a crossing path for critters on their way to the creek. The last thing I needed or wanted was to squash anything. Unless it was a mosquito or a blackfly.

Not knowing about the Oregon Trail for animals, Marilee kept up her speed and I lost her. By the time I shifted into high and came out on the trail by the cabin where the park rangers store their equipment, I saw her taillights up ahead. She was waiting for me at the bottom of the mountain. I pulled up alongside her and was about to say, "Ma'am, may I see your driver's license, please?" when I saw the amazement on her face.

"Look," Marilee whispered.

I looked far up into the sky and there they were. The lights the whole town had been buzzing about. Three white balls. They were in a neat row, and each one had flashing white lights beneath it. Then they disappeared.

"There they are again!" said Marilee. "Over there!" She didn't seem to be the Spineless Wonder now. She was more in awe than scared.

"Holy cow," I said. I, on the other hand, *was* scared. I was trying to find a flying wing or a crazy helicopter in the formations. Any explanation would do. The lights were now much higher in the sky over Allagash. Then, as if in a nanosecond from a distant world, they simply vanished.

"One thing is certain," Marilee said, breathless.

"What?" My voice had grown tiny with fright.

"This time, it's not your crazy brother."

could see wind beating the water down at Frog Pond. I hoped the frogs were using their lily pads as umbrellas. Every time we have a bad thunderstorm, Grandpa says it's global warming, and that the Air Force is behind it.

I dressed and went downstairs. From the kitchen window, I watched as rain beat on the tarred road and trees swayed low in the wind. Mr. Finley called to tell my mom that two of his chickens got loose and would we keep an eye out for them. Chickens hate thunderstorms. But after thirty minutes of booming and cracking and swaying, things calmed down a bit. Mom checked the weather report on her computer. While the thunderstorm was over, the rain wouldn't be stopping until 10 p.m. This wasn't good news.

Darn. I'd have to postpone a day, but that was okay. That happens in wars all the time.

"It won't kill you to stay in the house for a few hours," Mom told me. She unwound the cord to her vacuum cleaner and plugged the end into a wall socket. Now that the lightning had passed, I guess she didn't fear being electrocuted. "Read a book instead of playing games on your computer."

7

THE DELAY

I woke to the sound of rain beating on our shingled roof. The curtains were fluttering back and forth at my bedroom window. Wind shook the top of the oak tree in the yard, which I could see from my bed. I lay there, feeling safe from the storm, but thinking of what Marilee and I had seen the night before. Something just wasn't right. Much as I tried to do what Sheriff Mallory said, to find the logic in the mystery, I couldn't. What were those weird lights? How could they move so fast? How could they appear and then just disappear?

"Roberta, take the screen out and close your window!" my mother screamed up the stairs. "This is going to be a nasty one."

I removed the screen and shut the window. Then I crawled back into bed to think. The strange lights could have kept my brain busy, but I had more fish to fry, as Grandpa likes to say. *Roberta's revenge.* On my computer, I had already set up a fake e-mail account for Miranda Casey. I knew my brother would be too lovesick to notice when he received the e-mail. Instead of MirCase@mail.com, her *real* address, I set one up for MiraCase@mail.com. I was certain this would work.

Dear Johnny,

Please meet me TONIGHT after dark at the picnic table on Peterson's Mountain, near Calley's Creek.

I would, therefore, have a way to e-mail to Johnny from my computer with the same note that would go to her. As far as Miranda's message, all I had to do was sneak into Johnny's room again and send it from *his* computer:

Dear Miranda,

Please meet me TONIGHT after dark at the

picnic table on Peterson's Mountain, Calley's Creek.

There should be a sign on my door that says AT WORK.

Why did I want Miranda involved when I c this trick on just Johnny? I guess it had to do being so embarrassed in front of Billy Ferguso heard me say I like him, and from the top of Frog that. I wanted my brother to feel the same foolish front of Miranda. I know that Johnny is afraid of no matter how hard he tries to hide it. He can't watch a movie with a ghost in it. He might act all but if he ever saw a ghost on Peterson's Mountain, really freak out, even in front of Miranda. "You are su *girl*!" That's what I planned to yell at him as he ran d the mountain in the dark.

So my plan seemed fair enough to me. But it wa good thing I hadn't sent either e-mail yet since this w turning into the worst thunderstorm of the summer. went to my window and peered out at Mother Nature Lightning cracked across the sky. Thunder boomed. I

"You know what?" I said. "I think that's a great idea."

She gave me a suspicious look as I climbed the stairs. But when I heard the vacuum start, I knew her thoughts were back on the hallway carpet.

I locked my bedroom door and turned on my computer. Cell phones don't work in Allagash, as I mentioned earlier, so I sent Marilee an instant message. I didn't want either of our moms to overhear us on a land phone. Some people call this "eavesdropping," by the way.

AllagashRobbie: Plan delayed due to weather conditions! Will keep you posted.

Her answer came right back to me.

MeMarilee: Dad is coming for weekend. Bringing "she." Will not see you until Monday. Staying at motel in Fort Kent.

Now I was really disappointed, even though she'd be only twenty miles away. But she might as well be in China. It was Friday. I wouldn't see her until Monday. How many people would Johnny tell about Frog Hill as I waited? Damage control only works if you get on it right away. But at least it was summer and he wouldn't see most of our classmates until late August. And it seemed like Marilee's dad wanted to talk to her in person about his marriage plans. That was a good thing. Maybe "she" wasn't as bad as we thought.

Mom wanted me to read a book, so that's what I would do. Actually, I would read "about a book" until I visited the library to read the real thing. This was *The Allagash Abductions,* written by Raymond E. Fowler. He was the man who first hypnotized the Vermont Four and discovered they'd been taken aboard a spacecraft and examined. The morning after Grandpa's birthday party, when my family first saw the strange lights, I had called the local library and asked Mrs. Hafford to order it for me. And I also watched the YouTube video of the men on *Unsolved Mysteries.* This is what led to my awful dream of being examined by Dr. Bumblebee.

But I wanted to know more. Now that I'd seen the UFOs myself, maybe it *would* make a great science project. Marilee and I might finally win the Maine State

Science Fair. But as Dad often reminded me, a UFO is only an "unidentified flying object." It may not be from outer space at all, but from somewhere right here on Earth. I had even googled and found a photo of the Flying Wing. Uncle Horace was right. If I saw it even today, I'd think it was from Neptune.

I typed in "Allagash Abductions" and then clicked on the Wikipedia link. I settled down to read.

The incident started on August 20, 1976, when four men, all in their early twenties, ventured on a camping trip into the wilderness near Allagash, Maine.

I smiled. I mean, some towns are known for a brown ball of twine, the world's largest. And one town in Texas has the world's biggest cowboy boot. Bangor has Paul Bunyan. San Francisco has that bridge. I think it's kind of awesome that we are famous for our abductions.

The group consisted of twin brothers, Jack and Jim Weiner, their friend Chuck Rak, and their guide, Charlie Foltz.

"Weiner" must have been a tough name to grow up with. Kids can be so cruel. I imagined the twins being teased about it on the playground at recess.

They say their first day went by without incident.

However, on their second night, they noticed a bright light not far from their campsite which they first passed off as being a helicopter or a weather balloon, but later they noticed it displayed a strange quality of light. Suddenly, the object imploded and disappeared.

Well, there was Dad's helicopter and Mom's weather balloon. I guess it's human nature to look for a logical explanation. But a weather balloon didn't take these four men and examine them. A helicopter didn't gather hair and skin samples. Even though this event took place long before I was born, it's still talked about in town. After all, it happened right in our backyard, so to speak. Some people even spoke out publicly. For instance, Mr. Purdy, our principal, was once quoted in the school paper giving his own explanation. "There is such a thing as false memory," Mr. Purdy said. "I have no doubt that these men believe they are telling the truth. But the subconscious mind is greatly influenced by what we see in movies and on television, or read in books. I suspect this is where their memories have come from."

I wondered if Mr. Purdy had seen the lights that so many others were seeing over the past week. And, if so, did he fall into the helicopter or weather balloon group? After looking up the word "imploded"—it means to collapse inwardly, by the way, to disappear—I went back to Wikipedia.

Jack Weiner was the first to start having nightmares. In these dreams, he saw beings with long necks and large heads. The beings had large, metallic glowing eyes with no lids, and their hands were insect-like, with four fingers.

I'm not sure if cats have a sense of humor. They seem to. Sometimes, I'll look up from my homework or from eating a banana or watching a TV program, and my cat, Maxwell, will be staring right at me, the silly human. This was one of those Max moments. Just as I was reading about the glowing eyes and the four-fingered hands, Max jumped from the top of my bookshelf, where he likes to sleep, and hit on my desk. It was a perfect landing on all four feet. Have you looked at a cat's eyes recently? Slanted. Narrow. Glowing. They are eyes that belong to aliens.

After I scooted Max out the door and watched him slink down the stairs, I went back into my room and waited for my heart rate to go back to normal. That's when I heard an instant message arrive from Marilee. Her instant-message sound effect is that of a rooster crowing. I leaned in closer to read what she had sent.

MeMarilee: OMG!!!! TURN ON YOUR TV!!!!

I clicked on the small TV set I kept on a stand at the foot of my bed. I felt my mouth drop open. What was happening was a case for the record books, no doubt about it. Mom should see this too! I raced downstairs and pulled the cord on her vacuum cleaner. Then I turned on the large TV in the living room and hit the record button so the program would tape. Mom and I sat on the sofa and watched together, amazed. If I live to be a hundred years old, I don't think I'll ever be that surprised again.

"We'll wait for the others," Mom said. But I think it was more because she just didn't know what to say. She needed time to think, and so did I. So Mom went back to vacuuming, and I took Tina into the den to play with her doll. We knew the family would be coming by later for some Friday-night fried chicken, Mom's specialty. This would give us all a chance to "chew the cud," which is what Grandpa calls a discussion.

And that's just what happened, with Grandpa and Grandma arriving first. Then Johnny stomped in, hungry as usual and acting like he owned Microsoft or something. Billy Ferguson was with him. Billy actually smiled at me, as if maybe he knew I was alive and on the planet. It even seemed like a genuine smile. But then my logic kicked in. I figured he was still laughing over what I'd said about dating him one day. So I pretended I didn't notice he was in the room. Uncle Horace, who owns Horace's Auto Repair, and Aunt Betty, a hairdresser, arrived next. Once Dad was home from his woods job, we all sat in the living room as Mom played the recording of the five o'clock news.

This time, the cameras were in front of Sheriff Mallory's house and the reporters were crowded onto his front porch. One was even sitting in Mrs. Mallory's wicker rocking chair. They were talking loudly, waiting for the sheriff to come outside. Even Joey Wallace was there, making faces at the camera and grinning like a fool.

"Maybe this is what Hollywood stars have to put up with," Grandma said. "But we're in Allagash, Maine."

"They know a good news story when it comes along," said Uncle Horace. "It's their job."

Sheriff Mallory was now opening his front door and coming out to talk. I knew it wasn't possible, but he looked even more sad and tired than when Mom and I watched earlier.

"Ladies and gentleman, I have a statement to make," he said, "I did *not* see a UFO."

"Is it true that you gave the mayor an official letter retracting your sighting?" asked Andrew Birden, of *Fiddlehead Focus.*

"That would be correct, Andrew," said Sheriff Mallory. "After thinking it over, I believe what I saw was a formation of several airplanes from the base over in Burlington, Vermont." Then, he turned and looked directly into the camera, as if talking to us citizens and not the reporters.

"Folks," he said, in that down-home way of his, "I realize now that I'm in need of a vacation. I haven't had a decent one since Emma made me take her to Disney World back in 1994 so she could hear those singing bears." He smiled, but no one smiled with him. "Therefore, I have resigned as your sheriff, effective at noon today."

A bunch of questions came at him from the reporters.

But Sheriff Mallory went back into his house and closed the door.

"Like riding into the sunset," I said sadly. I liked Sheriff Mallory. He found Maxwell for me once at the top of an apple tree on Mr. Finley's property. He even borrowed a ladder and got Max down.

"Well, I never," said Grandma. "That's not the Stanley I know."

"Even if there's a logical explanation for what the sheriff saw, I don't doubt that he saw it," said my dad. "Someone obviously got to him."

"The mayor probably," said Grandpa. "Local Chamber of Commerce too."

"They don't want to scare tourists out of canoes and off snowmobiles," said Uncle Horace.

And then, as if on cue, our mayor appeared on TV. The cameras were now at his office for his comment. First, he thanked Sheriff Mallory for all his years of community service.

"I also want to reassure everyone, especially our visiting tourists, that Allagash is the safest town in Maine," said the mayor. "This is the perfect place for your vacation."

"What did I just say?" asked Uncle Horace.

"Those abductions back in 1976 didn't hurt our tourism here one bit," said my dad. "Heck, we should put up a big sign marking the site. It might help."

And then everybody started talking at once.

I slipped out of the living room and into the kitchen. I opened the door to the mud room and found my yellow slicker. I pulled it on and put my hood up. In the backyard, I plopped down on one of the cast-iron chairs at the cast-iron table near the fireplace. The fireplace now held wet, black ashes and remnants of burnt wood from Grandpa's birthday party, the evening my family first saw the lights. It was only three nights ago, and yet it seemed a lifetime.

Rain was still falling, but I didn't care. Something just wasn't right. My heart felt like it was made of cast iron. It's that feeling I get when I think the adults are hiding something from me. Or worse yet, telling me lies, such as when I found out there was no Tooth Fairy. I believed in her so much that I let Johnny pull my first loose tooth with a string tied to his bedroom doorknob. But at least I earned a dollar for my trouble. And Johnny seemed to really enjoy slamming that door. I lost four more teeth and earned another four dollars before Tommy Connors told me that the Tooth Fairy didn't exist. I asked my mother if it was true, and she admitted it. There was no Tooth Fairy. I remember what I said to her that day. "Then why did you tell me there was?"

If the Tooth Fairy could go down in flames *that* fast, the Easter Bunny didn't stand a chance.

So who was telling the truth now? The mayor or the UFO expert who wrote the book? The four Vermont men or the United States Air Force? Sheriff Mallory or Principal Purdy? Uncle Horace or Mrs. Cramer? I looked up into the gray and rainy sky and wondered if there were such things as stars. Would they shine again tonight, once the rain stopped and it grew dark enough to see them? Or had I just imagined them? Was everything I had ever believed in my life just one big lie?

Sometimes, kids have good reasons to mistrust the alien world of adults.

8
THE RUNAWAY

It was the longest weekend in recorded history. For one thing, the whole town had lit up with gossip about Sheriff Mallory's resignation, and what he did or didn't see that night on Highway 42. Most people figured the mayor was behind it, and the Chamber of Commerce was behind the mayor. Sheriff Mallory wasn't saying anything, but his wife, Emma, was. She told Aunt Betty, as Aunt Betty was cutting her hair, what Mr. Mallory said when he came home after resigning. "I love this town too much to hurt its economy. We're hanging by a thread as it is." A group calling itself "Bring Back Sheriff Mallory" had already formed and was making big plans. But first, they would have to hold a chicken stew and baked bean supper to raise the money they'd need for posters and bumper stickers.

I tried to stay out of the way as I waited for Monday and Marilee. On Saturday, I helped Mom sweep the basement. I even tidied up my bedroom, cleaned out my aquarium, and then fed my fish. Ever notice how fish have eyes like aliens? Lidless and glowing. Needless to say, I was imagining those eyes everywhere. And speaking of fish eyes, when I biked over to the grocery store to pick up a loaf of bread for Mom, I ran into the 4 Hs of the Apocalypse: Henry Horton Harris Helmsby.

"Hey, Henry," I said. He was standing in front of the aluminum foil as if maybe he had invented it. I figured he needed it to wrap up a poturn and see if it would bake, rather than blow up. After that night on Frog Hill when Marilee and I saw the fake alien, I had boycotted aluminum foil. So I was anxious to get out of that aisle.

"Good afternoon to you, Miss McKinnon," Henry said. He talks like that. He really does. If he were older and taller and had bigger teeth, Henry could be Barnabas on *Dark Shadows*. "A very rainy afternoon it is too," he added.

"I'm just getting a loaf of bread for my mom," I said, and tried to step past him. But he shuffled his skinny

body backward like a crab and blocked my way. I waited
for him to push his big, round eyeglasses up on his skinny
nose. They were always sliding down to his nostrils.

"And how might your science project be advancing,
pray tell?" he asked. "I have heard news that you and
the girl from Boston—what's her name, Marilyn?—have
joined forces. A wise idea, indeed, for you will be able
to rely upon the maxim that two brains are better than
one. But, of course, it all depends on *who* owns that one
brain." God, it's like someone created him in a laboratory
and then cranked his key and set him loose.

"Her name is Millicent," I lied. "And she's been living
in Allagash for almost a year now. Surely you noticed her?
She lives next door to you." *Dork.*

"Ah, yes, the young female next door who is always
spying on me," said Henry. "I believe I have noticed her.
She should wash her bedroom window. I predict she'll
have a better view of my greenhouse that way." *Moron.*

"Well, you have a good shopping experience, Henry,"
I said. "I gotta go." A crab-like leg spiraled out and again
blocked my path. It had a foot attached to it. The foot
was wearing a raggedy pink sock and a thick brown shoe

with black laces. The pants were green polyester and possibly came from his grandmother's dresser drawer. The sock, I would assume, belonged to somebody's Barbie doll. No one had ever accused Henry of being a slave to fashion.

"I wouldn't mind hearing about your project, Miss McKinnon," Henry said, but it sounded more like hissing. "That is, if you'd be willing to share details with a fellow scientist." I smiled my perfect fake smile, the one I created the first day I met Henry Helmsby.

"Actually, Millicent and I are keeping our project a secret," I said. "But I understand yours is a marriage of the Maine potato and the red turnip. I'm sure they will be very happy together. I give you my blessing." I imagined just then a potato and a turnip on the top of a wedding cake, instead of the usual little plastic bride and groom.

Henry's tiny eyes got beadier when I said this. His skinny neck turned his head so that the eyes could look right at me.

"The turnip is very historic," said Henry, all important, like he was Gregor Mendel or something. Henry once wrote a book report on Mendel's life, and his report was fifty pages longer than the actual book! "Early colonists brought it to the New World in 1609. It's a member of the *Brassica* family."

"No kidding?" I said, my eyes all glassy with boredom. "Well, I'm a member of the *McKinnon* family and I better get home before my supper gets cold, or Mom will kill me."

As I hurried down the aisle, I imagined my reflection caught in the lenses of Henry's large spectacles.

★ ★ ★

Sunday afternoon and night dribbled by slowly and painfully like the *drip-drop, drip-drop* of a leaky faucet, taking forever and driving me insane. At least the rain finally stopped. But without Marilee, my plan was still on ice. Finally, around five o'clock in the afternoon, I sent Marilee an instant message. I figured she would have her laptop at the motel. As much as it killed me, I hadn't contacted her since Friday night. I hoped she could concentrate on visiting her dad and possibly even liking his girlfriend.

AllagashRobbie: How's it going?

I'd forgotten about the message and was playing Spider Solitaire when the rooster crowed and a reply zinged back to me.

MeMarilee: I hate her!
AllagashRobbie: Give it time. Hang in there.
See you soon. Tomorrow night: Peterson's
mountain!

When she didn't reply, I figured they'd probably gone out for supper, or "dinner" as they would be calling it, confusing the local waitresses.

I can't tell you why, but I hate Sundays. Everyone just seems to wander around like chickens without heads, waiting for school or work on Monday morning. So I got into bed early, flicked on my TV, and found *America's Got Talent.* I watched a really cool kid dance. He was cute too. He looked a lot like Billy Ferguson, dark-haired and dark-eyed. Since that fiasco on Frog Hill, I had tried not to think of Billy in the way I often did. Sometimes, I would imagine him roaring into my yard on his four-wheeler, and instead of asking for Johnny, he'd say, "Is Roberta busy? Can she come riding with me?" And I'd put on my Fly helmet, which is pink and gray and white and has the word "FLY" written on it. I'd jump on the machine behind Billy and wrap my arms around his waist. Then off we'd go across the meadow, making all the frogs jump into Frog Pond.

As it stood now, the only thing I had my arms wrapped around was the extra pillow on my bed. When the show finished at ten o'clock, I saw that the rain had stopped. Through the curtains in my window I could see the planet Jupiter and almost make out a few of its moons. With binoculars, I can find three of the moons. It gave me goose bumps sometimes to think of how big and wide our own galaxy is. Mrs. Dionne, our science teacher, says that most astronomers don't question if there *is* life elsewhere in the universe, only *where* it is. That's pretty awesome.

★ ★ ★

"Roberta Angela?"

My mom was knocking on my bedroom door and

sunshine was spilling in through the windows. I squinted at my watch. It was almost eleven o'clock. I'm usually up long before this, but with school out, I guess my body was catching up on sleep.

"What is it?" I asked.

"Can you come downstairs, please?"

Mom doesn't use my middle name very often. She usually does it when she's sad or has something unpleasant to tell me. Maybe she's just heard a song on the radio by some guy named Bruce Springsteen, and it reminds her that her youth is slipping away. Or maybe the person she is cheering for on some reality show just got kicked off the island. Or she's just watched that same old, sad movie where Ingrid Bergman gets on the airplane and leaves Humphrey Bogart behind, wearing that dumb hat he wears. I can almost recite that stupid movie by heart.

"Roberta Angela?"

"I'll be right down," I said. I dressed in jeans and a yellow shirt. I knew what to do if it was *Casablanca* again. I'd sit next to her on the sofa and pat her on the back. "Listen, kid," I'd say. "If that plane leaves the ground and you're not on it, you'll always regret it. Remember, we'll always have Paris." That makes her laugh out loud. But it also means she will then have to hug me and say how much she loves me and how happy she is to be a mother. *Wow, Mom, write it down and e-mail it to Hallmark. Let them put it on a greeting card.* I don't say that to her, of course. I'm patient with my parents. They're human too.

But this time, Mom's face didn't look like any of those things I mentioned.

"What's wrong?" I asked. She came and put her arms around me.

"Honey," she said, "Marilee is missing."

When the room quit spinning around, I asked Mom some questions. Marilee had disappeared, or so I learned, sometime before 8 a.m. that morning. I remembered her instant message of the night before. *I hate her.* When Mr. Evans knocked on her motel-room door to wake her, she wasn't there. The bed had been slept in, however, so he assumed she stayed in the room last night.

"His hope is that she went shopping and will turn up at any moment. He called to see if you had talked to her lately."

I shook my head and said nothing, not yet, about the message or her feelings about the wedding. I knew she hadn't gone shopping. Marilee and I aren't the kind of girls who can spend hours at the mall trying on clothes we won't buy. And where would she shop at 8 a.m.?

* * *

By noon, when there was still no sign of Marilee, her parents contacted the Fort Kent Police Department and began driving the streets, hoping to find her walking around town. Since it was also possible she had found a ride back to Allagash, it was decided that Mom, Johnny, and I would search here. Dad had already gone to work. So we spent the next few hours searching everyplace we hoped she might be. The library. The school gym. Our two favorite rocks by the river. Her mom's toolshed, her mom's cellar, her mom's attic. I even rode the four-wheeler over to Mr. Finley's barn and asked if I could climb up into the hayloft and search through the hay piled there. A couple times before, Marilee and I had gone up there just to lie on our backs and smell the sweet smell.

Marilee Julia Evans was nowhere to be found.

By the time Mom, Johnny, and I got back home, I was

exhausted and heartbroken. Was my best friend okay? Sure, we have no serial killers this far north, but there's a first time for everything. And then, what if she headed south? What had she told me that night on Peterson's Mountain? *Do you think if I ran away, maybe downstate somewhere, that they would get back together?* I hated the thought of it. No one wants to tattle on their friend. But I knew that if Marilee didn't turn up soon, I'd have to tell my mom what I suspected.

Before we could go inside the house, Catherine's car pulled into the drive, followed by a second car. I felt my heart rise up with hope. Marilee's dad was driving the second car and a brunette was in the passenger seat. But I soon saw that Marilee was in neither car. Catherine got out first and there was panic on her face. My mom hurried over to give her a hug.

"She's still missing," Catherine said. "I hoped she might have come back to Allagash. I thought if we drove back here, we might see her walking along the roadside. But there was no sign of her."

In the country, twenty miles of road is nothing when you're driving. Folks in Allagash are in Fort Kent almost every day, shopping or working their jobs. But if you're a kid who has run away, it's a good stretch. It's all two-lane road too, and easy to spot a pedestrian. So if Marilee *was* trying to walk back to Allagash—she wouldn't dare hitch a ride—she was obviously good at sneaking around and hiding out. The Air Force uses the word "stealth" for this kind of action.

"We'll find her, Cath," my mom said. "She'll turn up any minute."

Catherine looked straight at me.

"Roberta, do you have any idea where Marilee is?" she asked. Behind her shoulder, Mr. Evans appeared. With him was a very pretty woman dressed in blue jeans and a denim jacket. *She*.

"Or where we might still look?" asked Mr. Evans. He seemed on the verge of panic too. But you could tell he was holding it together for everyone's sake.

"Sorry," I said. "I wish I did." It was the truth, really. I had no idea where she was. Only *why* she might have run away. And everyone must have figured that out by now.

That's when Deputy Hopkins turned into our driveway, the tires screeching on his police car. It was a wonder he didn't have the blue light swirling and the siren blaring. Everyone in town knows that our deputy gets all excited if a skunk so much as raises its tail as it crosses the road. The door opened fast and out lurched Deputy Hopkins. Harold. Except, I forgot. It was now *Sheriff* Harold Hopkins, given that Stanley Mallory had resigned. But thank God it was only temporary. If Mr. Mallory never came back, surely the town would vote in someone more qualified than Harold. Mr. Finley's dog, Mutt, would be a better candidate.

"I've had no luck, Mr. Evans," Harold said. He must have gotten up before dawn and polished his new sheriff's badge. With the sun hitting it, it shone like a silver beacon. "My men and I have scoured this town, every picnic area, every parking lot, every rental cabin, you name it. If she left Fort Kent, she didn't come to Allagash."

Johnny caught my eye and shot me a "What an idiot" look. It almost made me smile. Even fearing for Marilee's safety, it was hard not to have fun with Harold. And then he went and said something really stupid, something Sheriff Mallory never would have said.

"I don't want to alarm you city folks," said Temporary Sheriff Harold Hopkins. "But there've been a lot of UFO sightings in this area. As a matter of fact, we're famous for abductions. So we can't rule that out where your daughter is concerned."

Even if Sheriff Mallory *had* seen a UFO, he'd never say that to worried parents! Wait until the mayor and the Chamber of Commerce heard about this.

Catherine gasped, and her hand flew up to her mouth.

"Well, of all the crazy notions," my mother said, putting her arm around Catherine. "Harold, I've known you to make some foolish mistakes as a policeman, but this takes the cake."

"Officer," said Mr. Evans. He was now very angry. "You had better concentrate on looking for my daughter in the logical places, unless you want to be hit with a lawsuit."

Harold turned a little pale. The only thing he'd ever been hit with was a *baseball*, when Lonnie Black struck a line drive to third base during the big Fourth of July game between the firemen and the police department. Instead of keeping his eye on the ball, Harold was looking at Myra Colburn, who was sitting in the bleachers and giving him the fake eyelashes. He was out cold for two hours.

"Sorry, folks," Harold said, putting his hat back on. "I was just trying to cover all the bases." *Bases.* He must have been remembering the Fourth of July game too.

"Idiot," I muttered, but it was under my breath. Mom would be mad if I was rude to an adult, even Harold. I went over to sit on the swing and wait to see what the adults would do next. To my surprise, *she* followed me.

"Hello, Robbie," she said as if she even knew me. "I'm Sarah. May I talk to you a moment?" I nodded that it was okay, so she sat next to me on the swing.

"We will find Marilee. I'm sure of it," Sarah said. "Thank God this isn't Boston but northern Maine. Or I'd be more worried than I already am."

"You're worried about her?" I asked. Sarah's eyes got all watery then. I assumed it was due to tears.

"It's not easy for any kid," she said. "I know because my parents divorced too. Sometimes, it still hurts when I talk about it."

"Wow," I said. I needed to be a better daughter to my parents.

"But her father and mother were already separated when I came into the picture," Sarah said. "And there's nothing I'd like any more than to be a good stepmother to Marilee. Will you tell her I said that?"

I nodded. Sarah patted me on the shoulder then and smiled.

"Now, to find her," she said.

***

By midnight I was still awake, staring out my window and wishing on every star I could see in the sky. There was still no word of Marilee. The local news carried the story, and we all prayed that would help us find her. I decided to sleep with my clothes on that night, even though my jeans were kind of dirty, just in case something happened. I wanted to be ready to run and hug Marilee if she was found. For the first time in almost a year, I fell asleep not knowing where my best friend was.

9
The Search

B y the next morning, the whole town had turned out to look for Marilee. And then the state police were called in. They figured it was a runaway case upfront, but in small towns like this, people and police still take the time to look. It's not every day someone goes missing. In fact, nobody *ever* goes missing.

I finally told my parents everything Marilee said, that if she ran away, maybe her mom and dad would get back together. I knew she'd feel obligated to do the same thing if I were the one who was missing.

"Could she have gone back to Boston?" my mom asked.

"I don't know why she would," said Catherine. "Her father is here in town. And she lost touch with most of the friends she had down there once she and Robbie became so close."

And then Marilee's mother got a phone call from a former neighbor from when she and Marilee first moved back to Maine. This was at an apartment building in Fort Kent where they stayed for a couple months until Catherine found a house for sale in Allagash. The neighbor had looked out her kitchen window and there was Marilee, swinging on the swings used by children who lived in the building.

"I saw the missing person story on the news," said the neighbor, a woman named Carla. "So I called out to her and asked her to come in, but she refused. I ran inside to get the phone and when I came back out, the swing was still swinging but she was gone. It's only been five minutes since she was here."

We knew where she was and that she was okay! At least she was still in a safe part of the country. Our hearts almost burst with joy, as much as some of the adults wanted to throttle Marilee. Funny how you can do that. You can pray with all your soul that someone is unharmed, *please,* and still alive. And then when you find out they are, you want to kill them. But I think everyone was mostly just relieved and happy, even though it wasn't over yet.

"I'll call the Fort Kent police," my dad said. He had stayed home from work to join the search. "I know Doody Michaud personally." So he called and explained to the chief of police what had just happened. He also told him what the women said Marilee was wearing—a green sweatshirt and blue jeans. "And she has her brown hair tucked up under a black bandana to hide it."

Now Fort Kent was buzzing like a saw. And, of course, everyone wanted to drive there as fast as they could to search for Marilee. So her parents and my parents and my baby sister and my big brother and a fiancé named Sarah all piled into my Dad's two-seater pickup truck and headed to Fort Kent. I didn't want to go with them. Something in my mind kept telling me to stay there at home, that I could do more good there, especially if she finally telephoned me. And then, if I *had* gone, I'd have had to sit on Johnny's lap or Marilee's dad's. Stay here at home, my mind whispered to me. So I stayed.

Fort Kent was beyond buzzing now. But by mid-afternoon, when my mom telephoned to update me, things hadn't changed. I was now sorry that I hadn't gone with them. By now, almost three hours had passed since

Marilee was spotted on the swing. Yet, no one in that town of 4,000 people had seen a young girl wearing a green sweatshirt. You almost had to be proud of her.

"Robbie, there's nothing you can do but wait," Mom said. "Take a shower and get something to eat from the fridge. I'll call you if there's any news."

I went upstairs to my room and slipped out of the jeans I'd had on since the day before. They were really dirty from the search. There was even some hay in my back pocket from climbing up into Mr. Finley's loft. I threw the jeans into my wicker laundry hamper and pushed open my closet door. I pulled a T-shirt from the top shelf and grabbed a clean pair of jeans. When I reached down for my leather sandals, I saw two red sneakers with white laces staring up at me. I didn't own red sneakers, period, let alone ones with white laces. Where the heck did *they* come from? I leaned in for a closer inspection. When I grabbed one of the sneakers I discovered, to my surprise, that it had a warm foot in it.

That's when I remembered where I'd seen the red sneakers before. I pushed through my clothes hanging on the closet rod. And there she was.

"Marilee Evans," I said. "You come out of my closet and you come out *now*!"

Her face was pale and streaked, so I knew she'd been crying. Her bottom lip was trembling.

"I'm sorry, Robbie," she whispered.

Mad as I was, I threw my arms around her and hugged her tight.

"We've been so worried," I said. "When I first heard you were missing, I thought you had gone south and maybe a killer had picked you up."

"I wish," she said. "But you're right. I'm a big chicken. The Gutless Girl, remember?" She sat on the end of my bed and I sat next to her.

"You are none of those things," I said. "What you did was very brave." I waited for a drum roll that never came. "Brave and also very *stupid*."

"I know," she admitted. Then she sat wringing her hands as I called my mom pronto. Thank heavens her cell phone worked in Fort Kent. I heard Mom gasp and then cries of relief in dad's pickup as she told Marilee's parents. I hung up, knowing they'd be home in half an hour. I wanted that time to talk to my best friend.

"Where did you sleep last night?"

"In the big laundry basket they have at the apartments for tenants to use," said Marilee. "I covered myself with my jacket. No one ever goes into the laundry room before eight a.m. anyway. So I knew I could be gone by then."

"Where are your green sweatshirt and black bandana?" I asked, looking her over. Marilee stared down at the red blouse she was now wearing.

"When Carla spotted me on the swings," she said, "I knew she'd tell everyone what I had on. Carla has the biggest mouth in the apartment building. So I threw the sweatshirt away and just wore my blouse. And I got rid of the bandana too."

"If I ever plan to run away," I said, "I'd like for *you* to organize it for me."

"I must be in trouble so big it's invisible," said Marilee. "I feel foolish, Robbie. My poor parents."

"Why did you go swing there in the first place?" I asked. That part had really gotten my attention and I'd put a lot of thought into it, trying to figure out a method to her madness and, therefore, maybe find her.

"That swing is the last place I remember being truly

happy," said Marilee. "When Mom and I first moved up here, she and Dad were still together. She rented the apartment and started looking for a house. I thought we were all going to live in it. Then Dad drove up from Boston one weekend. He and Mom came out to where I was swinging in the yard and said they had to talk to me. That's when they told me the truth, that Dad wouldn't be moving into the new house after all. It felt good to be swinging there again. And then Carla Fowler saw me. Carla has eyes all over her head, like a housefly."

"Well, how in the world did you get *here* from *there*?" I asked.

"I ran from the swings at the apartment building and around the corner to the Irving Station. That's when I saw Mr. Hileman gassing up his truck there."

"Genius," I said. "You're a genius." I knew right away what this meant. Charlie Hileman wouldn't know if aliens landed on the roof of his rattling old truck. He was so out of touch that the transistor radio would seem like *Star Wars*. He lived alone on the other side of Peterson's Mountain in a little house in the woods. Folks in town claimed Charlie still thought John Fitzgerald Kennedy was President. Unless a neighbor told him—and his closest neighbor was two miles—he wouldn't even know Marilee had run away.

"I got a ride back to Allagash with Mr. Hileman," she said. "I told him Mack's Bike Shop was fixing my bike and I needed a lift."

I thought about this. My dad's pickup probably met Mr. Hileman's old truck on the road. My dad probably even waved at Charlie.

"Then I hid behind your mom's lilac bushes," Marilee continued, "until I saw you go out to the mailbox for the mail. That's when I sneaked in the back door and up the stairs."

"You've been in my closet for over two hours?" I asked, amazed. I could never stand still that long, not in a closet anyway.

"It felt like two days," said Marilee. "So what happens now?"

"Any second, you'll hear a pickup truck roaring into this yard," I said. "You will then go downstairs and out the front door. In the driveway you will find your mom, your dad, and a very nice woman named Sarah." It was an order, not a request.

"I can't, Robbie," Marilee said.

"Yes, you can."

"They'll ground me forever."

"Then I'll see you again when you're eighteen," I said.

Right on cue, I heard my dad's pickup truck pull into the drive, spraying the pebbles Mom had put down that spring, once the snow was gone for good.

I went to my bedroom window and peered down at the driveway. They were all piling out of the truck, like sardines from a can. And they were all talking nonstop. I turned and looked back at Marilee.

"Ready?" I asked, and she nodded.

"Ready," she said.

"Prepare to be hugged," I added, "before you're severely punished."

I stood at my bedroom window and watched the scene below. I figured Johnny would disappear before all the emotion started up, and I was right. He was nowhere to be seen. Marilee walked toward her parents with a straight and confident posture, which was a good sign. Although, I've read that Anne Boleyn did that same walk at the Tower of London just before they beheaded her.

I saw Catherine's face break into a big smile, her arms opening to her daughter. Then Mr. Evans hugged Sarah. And then Sarah and Catherine hugged. Then Sarah hugged Marilee. Then my mom and dad hugged Marilee at the same time. Then Mr. Evan hugged Sarah, and then Catherine. Then everyone hugged my mom. It was like watching *Wheel of Fortune*, when the contestant wins the money at the end of the show and their family and friends come running from the audience to rejoice with them.

I heard the bad news later from my mom. Marilee would be grounded for a month. No computer. And no social activities, which meant no Taylor Swift concert. Ms. Swift was playing at the Caribou State Fair and we'd bought tickets. If Marilee couldn't go, I would just give my ticket away. Going to a concert alone is like being one bookend. Taylor would just have to understand.

But a *month*, and in the middle of summer vacation? That's *forever* in my book.

We might as well have stayed in school year-round.

10
BACK ON TRACK

With Marilee grounded, my life was pretty much in limbo. I spent the next few days moping around the house, as Mom described it. On my fifth day of being friendless, I came to the conclusion that I needed a break from my own boredom. I looked at my bedroom clock. It was almost 11 a.m., and I knew what that meant over at Allagash Wood Products. Five minutes later, I was biking past the big sign near the main road that said *Picnic Tables, Lawn Chairs, Lumber, etc*. I was just putting the kickstand down on my bike when Grandpa came out of the main shop, carrying his black lunchbox.

"Well, look who's just in time to join me for a bite," he said. He sat in the shade on the front porch, in one of the sample Adirondack chairs that were for sale, and motioned for me to grab my own chair. I heard the familiar creak as he opened his lunchbox. Three or four times a month, if I found myself looking at the ceiling in my bedroom with nothing much to do, I'd bike over and have lunch with my grandfather. That's when he would tell me again about the olden days and the history of the big log drives that used to take place in Allagash. That's when lumberjacks would go into the woods in the autumns and stay in lumber camps all winter as they cut logs. In the springtime, they'd roll the logs into the Allagash River and follow them down to the sawmills where the logs would be cut into lumber.

"Millions of feet of lumber went down that river in the heyday of the big log drives," Grandpa would say, and the steady sound of his voice, as if it were the river itself, would bring the past back to me so fresh it was like it had just happened yesterday.

"Let's see what her note says today," Grandpa said, and found his eyeglasses in his shirt pocket. I took my submarine sandwich that I'd bought at Cramer's Gas & Movie Rentals out of the plastic bag that I'd tied to my handlebars. I pulled out the cold can of Coke and opened it. Then I sat on the shop's porch, in the shade next to Grandpa, and tore back the wrapping paper around my sandwich.

"When life gives you lemons," he read aloud, "make lemonade." He scrunched up the note and tossed it into the trash can by the side of the shop. "I wish life had given your grandma lemons and she had made me a nice lemon pie. Or maybe those lemon squares with the sliced almonds on top."

Grandma put a note with a positive message in every one of Grandpa's lunches. I know he liked the notes, even if he pretended not to by making light of them. Grandma told me that one day she forgot her daily message-in-the-lunchbox and Grandpa called her on his break, all upset and asking where his note was.

"First thing I do is to get rid of her vegetable garden," said Grandpa, as he picked the cucumber, tomato, and lettuce off his turkey sandwich. Grandma was doing her best to see that Grandpa ate healthy.

"She's just following doctor's orders," I reminded him.

"Well, she doesn't *have to*," said Grandpa. "It's not like she's in the Marines or anything."

"How old were you, Grandpa, when you went on your first log drive?" I asked.

"I only went on three before they stopped the drives altogether in 1963," said Grandpa. "I was fifteen when I went on my first one and seventeen on the last one. Some boys started even younger. It was the best way to learn, even though it was awful dangerous at times."

I knew this already, but I never grew tired of hearing Grandpa tell me. I also knew all about the log drives. There were lots of old photographs at the Allagash Historical Society and at the town library. Men wore red-and-black woolen jackets and corked boots. Some of them actually stood on the logs as they came downriver to stop them from jamming up. Now and then, an unlucky man went under the cold, swift water and never lived to see his next drive. But back then, the river was the only way to get those big logs down to the sawmills. Then the loggers started buying trucks and tractors and skidders, which had finally been invented. And before long, the log drives died away into history.

"Yup," said Grandpa as he finished a bite of his pure turkey sandwich. "I remember that last drive like it was yesterday. Spring of 1963. The older men, my father and uncles, they knew a way of life was gone for good. But that's the way the cookie crumbles." He pushed about in the paper towels Grandma had used to wrap his lunch.

"Speaking of cookies, I wonder if she broke down and gave me a molasses cookie for dessert," he said, his fingers searching. "God knows, I've eaten my share of yogurt and Jell-O. I'd like to sink my teeth into a big, fat chocolate donut right now or a piece of blueberry pie. They're in season now, you know."

"Chocolate donuts?"

"Blueberries," said Grandpa, a smile playing at the corners of his mouth. "You're starting to take after *me*, aren't you?"

I watched as he unwrapped a granola bar and then sighed, as if just the thought of blueberry pie might make him cry.

"It's not Grandma's fault," I reminded him. "Doctor Massey says your cholesterol level is way too high."

"He does, does he? Have you seen my doctor lately?" Grandpa asked, and it was my turn to smile. "I'd like to sit and watch *him* eat. I bet he's chowing down right now on my blueberry pie, and he'll wash it down with my chocolate donut."

"You're so funny," I said, still grinning. Doctor Massey was seventy-five pounds overweight if he was a pound. His belly even jiggled beneath his white lab coat.

"You'd probably need a stepladder to reach *his* high cholesterol," said Grandpa, and bit the end off his granola bar.

"Tell me again, Grandpa, about George McKinnon. I know it's a sad story, but I like hearing it."

"Well," said Grandpa, and shifted his feet the way he always did, resting his elbows on the wide arms of the chair. I could smell the fresh pine smell and knew he'd made the chair just that morning. Allagash Wood Products built everything from local trees and were real careful about harvesting them. Even Martha Stewart had ordered a picnic table from them once. A reporter from the *Bangor Daily News* came and interviewed the owners about their famous sale. And then everyone went back about their business. That's how it is in small towns. Sometimes there's a flare-up of activity and excitement, such as the recent UFO sightings, and then folks just get over it and go on with their lives.

"George was your great-great-grandfather on your daddy's side of the family," Grandpa was saying now. "He married a pretty girl named Sarah Gardner in the summer of eighteen hundred and sixty-five. That autumn, George left with the other lumberjacks to go up to the lumber camps in the woods above Allagash Falls. They would spend the winter up there cutting logs with crosscut saws and hauling them out to the riverbank with teams of workhorses. That's how it was done back then. No cars, no phones, not even a postal service. Those camps were far up the Allagash River where the biggest spruce and fir and cedar were growing. So there was no coming and going for visits with family. The loggers stayed up in the woods until spring arrived and they came out with the logs, driving them downriver."

"And that's why they called it a *log drive*?"

"You got it," he said. "You're turning into a regular genius, you know that?"

"So George McKinnon didn't see Sarah all that long winter?" I asked. I knew the story well since Grandpa had told it to me many times. I just liked to let him know I was still listening and still curious about the olden days.

"Nope," said Grandpa. "He never saw hide nor hair of her."

"So what happened that spring of 1866 when he finally came down the Allagash River with the logs?"

"Well, the first thing all the menfolk did, of course, was to make a beeline for home to say hello to wives and parents and children if they had them. Only, when George got to his house, he was met by some very sad faces."

I felt my eyes water. No matter how many times Grandpa told me this family history, the ending always caught me off guard. I didn't ask, "What happened then, Grandpa?" I had such a big lump in my throat that I couldn't say the words. I just sat there on the shady porch in the smaller Adirondack chair made for children and waited for the words to come to me.

"It seems that his beloved Sarah, his bride of just the previous summer, had realized she was expecting a child not long after George left that autumn. Before the river broke free of its ice that spring, just a couple weeks before the log drive would start down with the logs, bringing the men home to Allagash, Sarah McKinnon went into labor. But it was a hard one, and there was no doctor nearby, just midwives who did all they knew how to do. But that wasn't enough. Sarah Gardner McKinnon and her newborn baby girl both died. By the time George McKinnon opened the door to his house and announced happily that he was home, his wife and child were already in the cold, hard ground."

I wiped the warm tears from my eyes, then shoved the last of my sandwich back into the plastic bag that said CRAMER'S GAS & MOVIE RENTALS in big red letters on the front. I tried not to think of what George McKinnon must have felt that sad day so long ago.

"Now, remember the rest of the story before you go boo-hooing and scaring all the customers away from this shop," said Grandpa. I did my best to smile. "Don't forget that five years later George married a pretty girl with long brown hair named Mary Jane Hafford, who would become your great-great-grandmother. He married her and they had a lot of children. One of them your great-grandfather, Tom. That's how you're here, honey. You're here because that sad incident happened in the first place. Ain't it strange how life can be?"

"I don't care," I said. I didn't. Sometimes, when I

listened to the story, I would gladly give up ever being born just so Sarah and her baby girl could have lived. "Besides, if we weren't born, we'd never know it anyway. We wouldn't miss a thing."

Grandpa smiled. "Know what I admire about you, Robbie?" he asked. He was looking at his watch now and I knew that meant his lunch hour was over. "I like that you don't run from the hard facts of life. You keep asking me to tell you that story, even though you know Sarah and the baby aren't going to make it, no matter how many times I tell it. I can't change the past. But still, you want to hear the truth of that day. That takes courage, honey."

And then he ruffled the top of my hair with his big hand, which I have always hated. I leaned in close, asking for his arms. That was the time, at the end of the story, that I really wanted to let loose and boo-hoo, as Grandpa calls it. I wanted to boo-hoo so loud I'd scare the daylights out of all the customers who might be driving up to the shop to buy a birdhouse or a kitchen stool or a canoe seat. I didn't even care if one was Martha Stewart herself. But before I could cry, Grandpa did what he always did just then. He locked his arms around me and let me lie against his chest, smelling the sweet smell of his Old Spice aftershave, which comes in a white bottle with a little red clipper ship on it. He let me sink into the safety of his arms and be thankful that we were both born so that we got to know each other and share lunches and jokes and oral history every chance we got.

"Hey, you," said Grandpa, and lifted my chin so he could look into my watery eyes. "Would you do me a favor? Would you ride your bike over to Doc Massey's house and snatch what's left of my blueberry pie so I could have a bite of it for supper?"

By the time I was done laughing, Grandpa had closed his black lunchbox and snapped it shut. He'd thrown what was left of his granola bar out to the Canada jays and chickadees and grackles that always came around to see what the crew at Allagash Wood Products might be having for lunch.

Then Grandpa kissed me on my forehead and went back to work.

***

Time crept on like a snail or an inchworm, slow as cold molasses. I felt like I was in a glass jar, looking out at the world as I waited for Marilee's freedom. It had been two weeks since she'd run away and still I had heard nothing from her. I could only hope her parents would let her instant-message in a year or two. Maybe even attend school. But it was becoming apparent to me that I'd have to carry out the Peterson's Mountain plan all by myself. And I didn't like that idea. First of all, I missed not seeing my best friend. Second of all, I'd have to turn the fishing lantern on before I stood up and presented my ghostly self. Part of me, if the truth was told, was still a bit peeved at what Marilee did. I didn't blame her parents for putting on the ball and chain. But it added a big ball and chain around my own ankle as well.

The need for revenge, however, rarely goes away. Sometimes, it even grows larger. And mine had grown larger, like a giant *poturn,* as the days passed. Finally, I could stand it no longer. I folded Mom's white nightgown and laid it on my bed. I grabbed a hand towel from my bathroom and put it on top of the gown. Down in the toolshed, I rummaged until I found the fishing light.

I checked to see if it needed new batteries and it worked fine. But I'd bring a couple extras just in case I needed them. I had to think of everything, especially now that I was thinking alone.

In Mom's bedroom, I found the plastic case full of theater makeup that she used when the local college did *Our Town*. Mom always volunteers to paint backdrops and put makeup on the actors. I get my artistic flair from her. It's what my dad calls "being overly dramatic." The white facial paint was perfect. But when I saw the wig with its long brown ringlets, I knew I'd struck gold.

In my room again, I shoved the props into my backpack. If I wanted both of my victims on the mountain after sunset, I needed to be up there myself by six thirty. I looked at the clock on my desk. Still just 3 p.m. This was a good time to send the e-mails. I sat at my computer and pulled up the note to my brother from MiraCase@mail.com.

Dear Johnny,

Please meet me TONIGHT after dark at the

picnic table on Peterson's Mountain, near Calley's Creek. PLEASE do not tell anyone or it will spoil my plans! I have something IMPORTANT to tell you. Tonight's the night! Keep this secret, okay? I know I can trust you.

Always, Miranda.

It was with pure glee that I hit Send. I remembered how Billy Ferguson had smiled at me, sarcastically it seemed, as we listened to Sheriff Mallory say he hadn't seen a UFO. I could thank my brother for that.

"We'll see who's smiling now," I said. I hit Send again, and my e-mail to Miranda—or rather "Johnny's" e-mail to her—flew out into cyberspace.

Dear Miranda,

Please meet me TONIGHT after dark at the picnic table on Peterson's Mountain, near Calley's Creek.

Even though I knew she wasn't allowed on her computer, I sent Marilee a message, just to keep her informed.

> **AllagashRobbie:** Tonight is Roberta's revenge on Peterson's Mountain. I'll miss you. But the Lone Ranger rides again!

At six o'clock I was ready to go when I heard the rooster crow. I ran to my computer, thankful Marilee hadn't been sent to reform school, at least not yet.

> **MeMarilee:** Roberta's revenge or bust!!!!

I typed an answer fast.

> **AllagashRobbie:** What do you mean?
> **MeMarilee:** I am free!!!!!!!!!
> **AllagashRobbie:** OMG!! What???
> **MeMarilee:** Is there room for me on the back of your 4-wheeler?
> **AllagashRobbie:** OMG!!
> **MeMarilee:** I'll explain when I see you.

"Stay out of trouble, and for heaven's sake, don't run away!" Mom shouted, as I bounded down the stairs and out the front door.

I flew into the yard at Marilee's house as if someone had shot me from a cannon. I had tied an extra helmet to the seat, and by the time Marilee ran to the four-wheeler, I was holding it out for her.

From the front porch Catherine was smiling and waving to us. I wheeled around, with Marilee sitting behind me, and headed back in the direction of Peterson's Mountain. But first, I took the meadow path to the bottom of Frog Hill. I put the machine in gear and shut the engine off. Marilee jumped off and so did I. I grabbed her by the shoulders so I could peer into her eyes.

"Tell me what happened and tell me now!" I demanded.

"It's so amazing," she said. "They finally forgave me. I'm getting a second chance 'due to the circumstances,' as Dad called it. So they chopped two weeks off my sentence, and it's all thanks to *she*. You know, Sarah."

"What? Do not make me beg, Marilee!"

"Sarah told my mom and dad how tough it was for her as a kid when her parents went through a divorce. No one would even discuss it for years and years. Sarah says she wishes now she had thought of running away, that maybe then her parents would have been forced to talk to her about it."

"If I live to be a hundred and ten," I said, "I'll never be more shocked than at this moment."

"Oh, I bet you will," Marilee laughed. "Knowing *you*."

I jumped back on the four-wheeler and Marilee slid on behind me.

"I like Sarah," I said.

"So do I," said Marilee. "Well, sort of."

"Are you ready for some excitement?" I asked.

"I've never been more ready in my whole life!"

After we put our helmets on, I whirled the four-wheeler around and headed back toward the trail.

"Peterson's Mountain, here we come!"

w's this?" asked Marilee, excitement in her voice.
lly did seem to be a girl reborn. A girl brave
 to take on the night. She leaned out from behind
e and snapped on the fishing lamp. She aimed its
 my direction. Just as I'd thought, from ten feet
t turned my white gown a ghostly blue. I fitted the
 to my head and fixed the ringlets on my shoulders.
 I held both arms out in front of me.

ou're the scariest thing I've seen since Jimmy Norton
ght his tonsils to school in a jar," said Marilee. "To
nest, Robbie, I'll be glad when this wild plan of
 is over."

'm sure Johnny will arrive first," I said. "We need to
 until Miranda gets here. When you see me nod, turn
he light."

We heard a four-wheeler coming up the mountain, the
ant buzz of its engine like that of a monster mosquito.
"Quick!" I yelled. "Places!"

Crouched behind the huge ball of brush and hold-
g my nightgown up so that I wouldn't trip, I waited.
re enough, the four-wheeler soon reached the top and
lled into the picnic area. Its engine died. Silence. I

11
CALLEY'S GHOST

The trees that grow on Peterson's Mountain are mostly
old growth and therefore towering and thick at the
base. In many places, they block the sun from ever shining on the layer of needles and leaves that carpet the
forest floor. No timber has been cut up there since Old
Man Peterson and his sons felled trees with a crosscut
saw and hauled them down the mountain with a team of
horses. Most of the mountain now belongs to the state
and is preserved from cutting.

Sometimes, if you're walking up to the top and you
stop to listen, it's as if the wind in the trees is whispering
secrets to you. You might even hear ghostly music, what
sounds like a lonesome fiddle playing. Before you think
it's a party going on in 1914, however, you might see
that it's one dead tree leaning on another and moving

back and forth in the wind. Nature's music. And you will remember that all the Petersons are dead and gone, their houses and barns disappearing into the earth.

That doesn't mean, of course, that there *aren't* ghost fiddlers up there somewhere in that dense forest of pine and spruce. Or dogs that disappear into thin air as soon as they reach the gate to the old Peterson cemetery. It doesn't mean that the mournful cry you hear through the pines at midnight is actually a screech owl, and not a dead ghost child weeping for its mother. Peterson's Mountain has seen it all. And each man, woman, boy, or girl who goes up there has to decide for themselves what is of this Earth and what isn't.

The park rangers must have thrown more dead branches and boughs onto the brush pile over the past few days because it looked bigger and fatter than when I first saw it. A hippopotamus could have hidden there. I parked the four-wheeler out of sight behind it and Marilee jumped off. She was already a different girl, or so it seemed to me. I hoped she and Sarah would have a good relationship now. At least, Marilee seemed happier. And I figured there was more behind the happiness than having her prison sentence chopped in two.

Johnny and Miranda woul either side of the picnic table from the brush pile. At that di any talented ghost can look.

"Here's the lamp," I said, and looked at my watch. Six-forty. Ti Johnny or Miranda arrived early. and dropped it on the ground be pulled out the white nightgown a my clothes. Then Marilee helped s cake makeup onto my face.

"How do I look?" I asked.

"Like someone named Calley wh 1914," said Marilee. "You're freaking

"This is gonna be awesome," I said place behind your tree." I watched as over to the scraggly old pine that grew t brush pile.

There was still plenty of sun down be that mountain, shadows were already flick were swaying gently. Another twenty m would be downright eerie.

"Ho
She rea
enough
the pin
light i
away,
wig or
Then,
"Y
broug
be h
your
"
wait
on
dis

in
Su
p

imagined Johnny sitting there like a duck on Frog Pond, waiting for his goddess to arrive. Or maybe Miranda was first. Who cared? Within seconds, another machine came buzzing up the mountain. I heard it circle the picnic area and then its engine also died.

"You got my message. Cool." Johnny's voice. It was time to act!

I nodded my head back and forth, knowing there would be just enough light for Marilee to see the movement. Then I stood up, both arms extended. Right on cue, the light of the fishing lamp hit me, my own personal spotlight. I had to be a sight to move the dead, so to speak. I decided to carry it a step further. I moaned, a long lamenting groan.

"Holy Moses! Look at that!" Johnny again. "What the H is that thing?"

I took a step forward, my arms reaching toward his voice. All I could see was the blue of the fishing light.

"It must be Calley's ghost!" A new voice. But it wasn't Miranda. A male voice. A familiar voice. Billy Ferguson! My brain raced. Where was Miranda? And then, my brain slowed back down. Scaring my brother in front of

Billy Ferguson was a B, not an A effort. But a B was better than a D or flunking altogether. I kept walking.

"Shoot it!" I heard Billy shout. "You got your gun, Johnny! *Shoot!*"

Huh? What? Did I hear what I just heard? Johnny did, indeed, have a .22 rifle that had once belonged to my dad. He wasn't allowed to kill anything but pop bottles and tin cans. And ghosts, I would think, if they were threatening his life.

I heard thrashing in the trees behind the old pine and realized that Marilee was running.

"*It's me, Johnny!*" I screamed. "*Don't shoot!*"

I didn't wait for the sound of gunshot, much less the bullet. With my nightgown hiked up to my hips, I followed Marilee into the woods, running wildly, branches and trees slapping my face. I didn't know which was worse, the thorns of the blackberry bushes when we ran from Frog Hill, or the heavy-duty pine branches that were now whacking me in the mouth. Behind, I could hear the hoots and whoops of laughter. Why was that wrong? Maybe I was running to avoid being wounded or killed. But Johnny should be running too, having just seen Calley Peterson's ghost. I stopped and tried to catch my breath. My blood was throbbing in my eardrums. Where was Marilee? I started running again, and that's how I found her *BAM!* when I plowed into her. The impact almost knocked us both down.

"I can't see a thing in front of me!" Marilee cried.

"Grab my hand," I whispered. "Go slow. One foot in front of the other. I'm pretty sure the path is to our right."

Marilee took my hand, and together we turned and walked four steps to the right. And then we were falling together, down, down, nothing but empty air and darkness below us.

12
MISSING TIME

I could feel Marilee lying on the ground beside me. But I couldn't see her. Wherever we were, it was in total darkness and it smelled damp, like a shaded riverbank. Moist black soil, that sort of smell. Maybe even a rotted-potato-sack smell.

"Are you all right?" I heard her ask.

"I think so. Are you?"

"I think so. My ankle hurts a little."

"Where are we?" I rubbed a lump on my forehead the size of a cherry.

"I don't know," said Marilee. "But I bet it's some old foundation of a Peterson house."

"Oh, no!" I said. "If Johnny doesn't come looking for us, we'll have to spend the night up here."

"I'll die. Do you hear me, Robbie? You'll never talk me into anything crazy again."

"That was Billy Ferguson with him," I said. "My plan must have had a hole in it."

"A major hole," said Marilee.

We heard voices from up above, getting closer.

"Here!" Marilee shouted.

I was just about to say, "Maybe we should spend the night here and not give Johnny the satisfaction." Then we were blasted with the beam of a flashlight.

"Look what I found, Billy," I heard Johnny say. I squinted up into the stream of yellow light. It seemed to be about ten feet above our heads. "We snared a couple rabbits."

"One rabbit has a really white face," said Billy.

I felt my shame grow larger and take deeper root.

"You okay down there?" Johnny finally asked.

"Yes," said Marilee. "Please, Johnny, get us out!"

"Hang on," he said. "Billy's gone back to the four-wheeler for a rope. Looks like you fell into an old well. Good thing it's dried up."

When Billy returned with the rope, it was thrown down to us.

"You go first," I said to Marilee. I felt I owed her that

much. I helped tie the rope around her waist and then the boys hoisted her up. I was next.

"Is that makeup, or are you just really scared?" Billy asked.

I said nothing as we followed them back through the woods, their flashlight lighting the way.

"Oh look, Roberta. Here's your hair," Johnny said. He shone the light on a mass of curly brown hair clinging to the branch of a spruce. I pulled the wig down. I wanted to say, "Hey, dude, what's that gap between your teeth? A parking space for a brown M&M?" But I didn't say it. The defeated should keep their traps shut. I remembered the sign I wanted to put on my door just hours earlier. GENIUS AT WORK. One word would need to be changed to IDIOT.

I grabbed the hand towel from my backpack and wiped off as much white makeup as I could. Then I stuffed the nightgown and wig into the pack. I threw the whole thing into the storage box of my four-wheeler.

"Your plan had one big mistake," said Johnny. "Miranda is at her grandmother's in Pennsylvania for a week. When I got that crazy e-mail, I called to ask her what was up. Guess what? She got one too. Good try, Robbie. It might have worked if you weren't such a girl."

He and Billy laughed. I got on the four-wheeler, threw on the headlights, and drove it out from behind the brush pile and over to the picnic table. Billy's machine was sitting there next to Dad's, which Johnny was driving. I braked and waited for Marilee to climb up behind me. I thought I saw her smiling, but I didn't want to go there just yet.

Billy got on his four-wheeler and the engine roared to life. He snapped on his headlights. Johnny was just packing up his flashlight. He obviously didn't have his rifle with him. Was there a bone left in my body that wasn't gullible?

"Just one more thing," Johnny said. "I think if Mom and Dad knew about this, they'd be really pissed. And they wouldn't be happy about Frog Hill, either. So I think we call it a truce, okay?"

I really wanted to cry. So much planning, so much effort, and all for nothing. I was about to say, "Okay, truce," much as it hurt, when I saw Johnny looking up. We all followed his gaze. In the sky above us, about a hundred yards up, a large triangular craft was hovering. Rows of white lights lit up its sides, much like what Sheriff Mallory had described. From the belly of the craft, beams of light were shooting down, moving back and forth, as if searching for something. Suddenly, one beam hit the ground in front of my four-wheeler. It moved back and forth, as if it might be heat-seeking. It would find us in no time.

"Drive, Roberta!" I heard Johnny scream. "Hide in the old cave!" I threw the machine into high gear. As I did, I saw Johnny waving the flashlight up at the craft, signaling it. "Hurry, Robbie! I'll come find you!" And then my brother turned and ran back to the brush pile. The beam of light that was sure to find Marilee and me now followed *him*. Oh, Johnny! I realized then that I'm a coward at heart. *I'm* really the Gutless Girl.

We flew down the mountain, Billy in the lead. I didn't pause a second at Rabbit Crossing and prayed nothing was there. About two-thirds of the way down, on the banks of Calley Creek, is a cave so well-known the rangers sweep it out so that people can have picnics in there. It's large and dry. We flew off the path and, one behind the other, our four-wheelers disappeared into its huge mouth. We snapped off our lights. From the cave's opening we could see the silver moon. It was a lot bigger than the fingernail it had been the night of Grandpa's birthday party. It was almost full now. We waited, breathless and frightened. Only moonlight lit the cave, but as our eyes adjusted we could make out each other's silhouettes.

"I hope he's okay," I whispered. A flood of tears was right behind my words. My big brother. My *only* brother.

"Johnny is so brave," said Marilee. He *was* brave. For all my life, I'll remember him waving the flashlight, signaling that weird craft to get its attention away from me, his *little sister*. He might be afraid of ghosts, but apparently he could take on UFOs any night of the week.

"Don't worry," said Billy. "He'll be here any minute. He knows this mountain by heart." I had to wonder why Billy didn't go running with a flashlight, luring the attention away from us. He had just lost a couple points in my eyes. But then, few people would do what my big brother did.

"Listen," said Marilee. "I hear something."

We listened as much as we could with hearts still beating loudly. It sounded like an engine of some kind.

"It must be him," said Billy.

"Oh, thank heavens," I said, even though I didn't trust the heavens at that moment.

In the moonlight, I saw Billy tilt his head to one side as he listened.

"That's Johnny, all right," he said.

And that's when the cave flooded with the most intensely bright light I'd ever seen. It was so bright that it was beyond white. I remember thinking, "That's no four-wheeler."

✳ ✳ ✳

We were sitting on our machines at the mouth of the cave on Peterson's Mountain. Me. Marilee. Billy. And Johnny. The moon was much higher now and brighter. The sky was filled with stars. Our machines were all running, headlights on.

"We'd better get home," said Marilee. "My mom is already as nervous as a long-tailed cat in a room full of rockers." I smiled. That was one of Grandpa's favorite sayings that Marilee had picked up. I looked over at Johnny and he was looking back at me.

"You okay?" he asked.

"Yes," I said. "Thanks for what you did back there."

"Yeah, dude," said Billy. "Thanks for that, man."

"You were so brave!" Marilee gushed.

"No biggie," said Johnny. But he was awfully quiet. So were Marilee and Billy. So was I, for that matter. I mean, it had been a hair-raising night in more ways than one.

"Let's get out of here," said Johnny. "The game is on at eight o'clock."

"It's ten," said Marilee, looking at her watch in the glare of Billy's headlights.

"What?"

"Huh?"

"It can't be."

Billy, Johnny, and me in that order.

"But it is," said Marilee. "Unless my watch is broken."

Billy stuck his wrist out where the light would catch the numbers on his own watch.

"A minute past ten," he said.

I looked at the Timex Sports Watch my mom had given me for Christmas.

"Ten o'clock," I said.

"Well then," said Johnny. "Definitely time to go home."

We followed Johnny the rest of the way down the mountain. At my house, Marilee jumped off from behind me and got on Billy's machine. He lived just past her house so he could drop her off.

"Good night," Marilee said.

"See you," I said.

"Take it easy," said Johnny. We stood and watched as their taillights disappeared. Then we turned and went into our house. Mom looked up from her TV show, surprised.

"The two of you together?" she asked. "What will my eyes see next? And why were you not home sooner, Robbie? It's past ten o'clock."

"Don't worry," said Johnny. "I was looking out for her."

"Yeah, I was fine," I said. "I was with my big brother."

Mom laughed out loud, thinking we were being sarcastic, as usual. She glanced over at Dad as if to ask if he'd heard this. But Dad was asleep on the sofa, his glasses resting on his chest.

"Good night," I said, and trudged slowly up the stairs. My legs felt as if they each weighed a hundred pounds. My arms at least fifty each. I was exhausted. I heard Johnny sigh as he climbed the stairs behind me and knew he was feeling the same way. At my bedroom door, I paused. Johnny walked past me to his own bedroom.

"Johnny?"

"I don't want to talk about it," he said. I nodded. He opened his door, but he didn't step inside.

"That was a brave thing you did tonight," I said.

"I wasn't brave," he said. "I was just scared."

"Scared of the UFO?"

"No," he said. "Scared something bad would happen to you."

I left my door and ran down the hallway and into his arms. He hugged me tight. That was the first time he'd done that since we were little kids. Maybe Mom was right. We would bond, Johnny and I, and be great friends for life.

"Now get some sleep," he said. I walked back to my room, my heart surging with love. "Pipsqueak," he added.

I slept that night as if I hadn't slept in fifty years. No dreams. No waking in the middle of the night when Maxwell stomped all over my pillow. No hearing Dad's pickup truck leave for work at 6 a.m. No hearing Mom get Tina up and bathed at 8 a.m. When I finally did wake, I was starving.

And I also had a lot of questions. What the heck happened to us on Peterson's Mountain?

13

THE DENIAL

The next thing the four men knew, they were back onshore at their campsite. They all felt exhausted and decided to sleep for the night. The large fire they had made only minutes previous was now just a pile of burnt embers. Without much conversation following the unusual incident which just took place, the men went to sleep. The next morning, they said little of the incident and packed their belongings to move to a new campsite.

I was back on Wikipedia, reading up on the Allagash Abductions. A full week had passed and yet Johnny, Billy, Marilee, and I had said nothing about what happened on Peterson's Mountain the night I dressed up as Calley's ghost. The night we hid in the cave. The night of the bright light that found us. You'd think someone would say, "Hey, remember that weird spaceship we saw? You know, the one that chased Johnny?" But no. It was as if something had been erased from our brains. I mean, I know we all remembered seeing it. Just as the four men from Vermont remembered seeing a ball of light. It's what happened *afterward* that I wanted to discuss. How else could we get to the bottom of things? But everything seemed to have quieted down all over town, not just with the four of us. No more sightings were mentioned and the strange lights everyone had been seeing had, well, imploded. Or they were invisible to us.

After psychiatric examinations, all four men were deemed to be mentally stable and they all passed lie detector tests. In 1988, out of curiosity, Jim Weiner attended a UFO conference hosted by Raymond Fowler. Fowler was excited about Jim's story, especially the fact that it was a multiple-witness occurrence. Fowler suggested to Jim that he and the others undergo hypnosis. After the sessions, it was revealed that all four men had memories of being abducted.

Well, we four would also be a multiple-witness deal if the other three would just talk about it. I didn't want to read on. I knew what it said, anyway. The examinations. Those hair and skin samples.

I heard the rooster crow. An instant message from Marilee.

MeMarilee: Want to go to Cramer's for an ice
cream?

I quickly typed back:

AllagashRobbie: No, but I want to talk about
what happened on Peterson's Mountain.

The rooster crowed again.

MeMarilee: We could have broken our necks.

My sound effect is a horse whinny. I imagined Marilee
hearing it over at her house as I typed back:

AllagashRobbie: I want to talk about it! ASAP!!!!

When there was no response after twenty minutes, I shut
my computer off. Out in the hallway, I met Johnny. He
had just gotten out of the shower and was pulling on a

clean T-shirt. I stepped in front of him, blocking his way to the stairs.

"Were we abducted on Peterson's Mountain?" I asked. It doesn't get any more to-the-point than that. At first, Johnny looked nervous, but in no time he was flashing his usual crooked grin.

"You crazy?" he asked. "If they took one, they'd take us all, right?"

"Right," I said. Absolutely. We had *all* lost two hours on that mountain. So how did that happen? And why was I the only one concerned?

"Well, there's your answer," said Johnny. "They'd be looking for intelligent life, right?"

"Most likely." I figured they would be examining all kinds of animals and probably even plants. I mean, who would notice if a tree was abducted from the Allagash wilderness?

"If they're looking for intelligent life, why would they take a blond?"

Oh, dude. Not the dumb blond joke. Get a new act, Johnny. He was being mean again, and so soon into our bonding, or whatever that was. My disappointment must have shown on my face because Johnny quickly tousled my hair.

"Let it be, Robbie," he said. "It's over and done with. I gotta go. Uncle Horace is picking me up in ten minutes." He was down the stairs before I could even reply.

In the kitchen, I poured myself a glass of orange juice. Mom came in with a bag of groceries and started putting them away.

"Do you believe in aliens?" I asked. "You know, beings that inhabit other planets?"

Mom gave me a sharp look. I knew it was because Tina was there, standing next to her and eating a Popsicle. Tina is shy in front of the milkman and the mailman. Spacemen would really terrify her.

"No, I don't believe in aliens," Mom said. "And now that things have finally quieted down, I don't want to hear about them, either."

Have you ever seen a photograph of an ostrich with its head in the sand? No, you haven't, because it's a myth that the bird does that when it senses danger. But if it did, I'd be living in a family of ostriches. Even my best friend had her head in the sand.

"What if they walk among us?" I asked. Tina had followed Maxwell into the living room. "What if Johnny and I are not really your children but were put here by aliens?"

"That I would almost believe," said Mom, "if my labor pains hadn't hurt so much."

★ ★ ★

I saw Dad trimming the hedges in the yard so I went out to pretend I was there to help him. He looked up and smiled when he saw me.

"How's my girl?"

"Dad, do you believe in aliens?" I asked. "Is there life on other planets?"

He stopped trimming to wipe the sweat from his forehead.

"There's a good chance, I suppose," he said, "what with all the stars out there that are like our own sun. Stars with planets of their own. But I doubt we'll know the answer in our lifetime, Roberta. Hand me that soda."

I handed him a can of Pepsi that had turned warm

in the sun. Was it so wrong to want answers now, in my lifetime? I was never big on waiting.

"Where does that leave God?" I had to ask it. I waited as Dad finished his soda and handed me the can. Five cents refund and he didn't have to remind me.

"Well," Dad said, as he went back to clipping, "if there is life on other planets, then maybe God created them too. It's just a bigger neighborhood out there than we realized, that's all."

That wasn't a bad answer. But I knew I had questions that even my dad would furrow his brow over. And that's what he did when I asked my next one.

"If there are UFOs flying over Earth, why don't they land and make themselves known? Why don't they share their technology with us?"

After the furrow came and went, Dad said, "Well, maybe they are so intelligent that we're like ants to them. You don't sit and talk to ants, do you, Robbie? Or, on the other hand, maybe they've seen MTV."

* * *

I gave up. In the front yard, Billy Ferguson was just pulling in on his bicycle. He popped down the kickstand and turned to look at me.

"Johnny here?" he asked. What an opportunity. Johnny had gone to Caribou with Uncle Horace for the day.

"He won't be back until this afternoon. Want to sit on the swing and talk?"

Billy looked nervous. Like I might grab him, pin him down, and kiss him to death. But we sat on the swing and Billy pushed us in motion with a foot. After we went back and forth, back and forth, he seemed more comfortable. That's when he said it.

"Maybe we can go four-wheeling sometime. Or ride our bikes over to Cramer's for an ice cream."

You would think, wouldn't you, that I'd smile when I heard this? Or maybe *swoon,* which is a word I picked up from one of Mom's old black-and-white movies. I think it means "to faint." I could have even gulped. But, no. Here's what I did. First, I blushed, which is something I wish I could control. I hate a blush. And being blond doesn't help hide it, let me assure you. Second, I was so nervous at what Billy just said that I simply blurted out my big question.

"What do you think happened on Peterson's Mountain the other night?"

You'd have thought I just clobbered him on the head with a poturn. His foot stopped the swing. He jumped off and went to his bike. He kicked up his stand and jumped on the seat. "I gotta go."

I watched until he disappeared down the road, an ostrich riding a bike. I had to hope that in the future I'd learn to be more careful. That way, maybe my boyfriends wouldn't run from me.

★ ★ ★

There was one person I thought might talk to me. I couldn't take the four-wheeler on the main highway, so I got out my bike, put on my helmet, and told Mom I'd be back in time for supper. I set off pedaling down through the modest gathering of houses, past the one grocery store and the small café, past the school and the police station, past the gas station and movie rentals, past the post office and the library, and then that was it. Town was over and I was pedaling out south into the "suburbs," so to speak.

I love my bicycle. Mosquitoes and blackflies can't catch you on a bike or a four-wheeler, which is a major perk. Manufacturers should put that in their advertisements: *This Schwinn Girl's Ranger bicycle is light blue, has knobby tires for traction, is mosquito-proof, and with its twenty-one gears can easily outrun blackflies.* Honestly, I think they would sell more bikes in the northern states.

I pulled into Sheriff Mallory's driveway and braked. As I was leaning my bike against his porch railing, the door opened and there was the sheriff. Or the *former* sheriff. He looked different without his uniform. He looked just like anybody's grandpa, in tan slacks and a white cotton shirt.

"Well, look what the wind blew in," he said, and beckoned for me to come sit in one of Mrs. Mallory's big rocking chairs on the front porch.

"Thanks, Sheriff Mallory," I said. "Well, Mr. Mallory."

He smiled sadly and nodded.

"It sure seems strange not to be the sheriff anymore," he said, and handed me a stick of gum. "But Harold will be a fine sheriff. He was an interesting deputy, I can say that much."

"He won't last a month, and you know it," I said. This

made him smile. He likes me, Mr. Mallory does. I know because I heard him telling my dad once at a school function. "I sure get a kick out of that girl of yours," he said. "It's like talking to a miniature adult."

"Well, let's just hope he doesn't do too much damage until a new sheriff is voted in," said Mr. Mallory. "You can call me Stanley now that I'm no longer with the department."

"I would like to know, Stanley, what you really saw on Highway 42 that night," I said. "I want to know because I think I saw it too."

Stanley Mallory looked me in the eye, steady and sure. He sighed as he ran a hand through this thinning hair. He looked tired. No wonder. He'd been through a lot lately. Our mayor wasn't an easy guy to deal with. So if he and the chamber were putting a vise grip on our sheriff, as everyone expected, it couldn't be fun.

"I didn't see anything unusual," he said. "Thinking back on it, I'd say it was several of those low-flying planes from the base in Burlington, Vermont. You've seen them, haven't you, Roberta?"

Yes, I'd seen them often. They flew over during the day and they looked like airplanes. So I told Stanley what

I'd seen. I even started with the ghost prank I was hoping to pull on Johnny, to explain what we were doing on Peterson's Mountain so late at night. Then I told him about Johnny signaling to the craft, and how we flew down the mountainside to the cave.

"The light that shone in on us was so bright we couldn't look at it," I said. "No way was that Johnny's four-wheeler."

Stanley Mallory sat in his rocking chair and stared out at his mailbox. It had two red cardinals on it, their feet grasping a brown twig. I figured Emma Mallory had painted it herself. She used to teach art at the high school and still gives lessons.

"That's quite a story," said Stanley.

"There's more," I said. "It seemed like just a second later that we were sitting there on our machines, Johnny too, at the mouth of the cave." I paused, since it still scared me to think about it. "But it was really two hours later."

"That's sure a wild tale, Roberta," Stanley said.

"Wild and true," I noted. "But you saw it too, didn't you?"

Stanley waited a bit before he replied.

"I saw a bunch of airplanes. Those jets fly like the dickens."

"What about the bright light that lit up Paul Ellory's dairy farm? It was so bright you could see Mr. Ellory's cows and his red tractor and his two silos. You said so yourself."

"It had been a long night," said Stanley. "I was tired, and when your eyes get tired they see all sorts of things."

We sat in our rockers, saying nothing. Cars and pickups and trucks went back and forth on the main road. I was getting my Tooth Fairy feeling again, no doubt about it.

"I'm on a team all by myself," I said finally. "I can't even get Johnny and Marilee and Billy to admit what they saw that night."

I stood up and shook Stanley's hand.

"Thanks for your time, Mr. Mallory," I said. I didn't feel like calling him Stanley anymore. I was too disappointed in him.

"I'm sorry, Roberta," said Mr. Mallory from his rocker on the porch. I was just kicking up the stand on my bike. "But I gotta think of our town. I gotta put Allagash first. One day, when you're older, you'll understand."

"I'd like to understand before I turn twelve," I said. "See ya, Mr. Mallory."

14
THE SIREN

The next day started off with a bang. There was some breaking news, and by this I mean *glass* breaking. Apparently Henry Horton Harris Helmsby, in his great attempt to join two vegetables that had been happy living apart for a few hundred years, blew up his mother's greenhouse. Glass flew so far that some of it ended up on Marilee's lawn. Poturns littered the road in front of Henry's house, and now Maggie Dunn's chickens were pecking at the pieces and in danger of being flattened by pulp trucks.

The incident was important enough that at last Marilee e-mailed me. Attached to her e-mail was a photo of shards of glass sticking out of her mother's rosebush. Another photo was taken from her bedroom window and was of the greenhouse itself, which now looked like a giant mushroom had exploded. The trouble with Henry was that he had about three really bad ideas until he came up with a brilliant one. And that's what worried me. In the past, he had always rooted up a gem in time for the fair. Such as the potato battery that could power a digital clock. Or the solar oven made inside an oatmeal box that could fry an egg. And he always won.

I went on our school's Facebook page and saw a photo of Henry. It was posted by Mrs. Dionne, our science teacher, in the hopes that his classmates would offer him their condolences. So far, only Mrs. Dionne had posted anything. *Get well soon, Henry*, was all her message said. And then Henry's little sister, Pearl, had posted something too. *My new Barbie doll is missing! It better not be because of you, Henry!* I didn't even want to remember the time Henry got involved with a Barbie doll project. It had to do with Barbie's fibers. Or rather the synthetic fibers her hair is made from. But I'll save that story for later when I have the stomach to tell it.

I guess Henry's mother took the photo of him. His cucumber face was all wrapped up in a white bandage, enough that just his beady eyes were peering out. I figured if you undid the bandage, the face beneath would now look like a toasted Tootsie Roll. Below the photo, Henry had offered these words of wisdom for the world: *This accident will only make me stronger. I suspect that great botanical minds before me have also blown up their moms' greenhouses. If the* Brassica *family does not wish to join the* Solanum *family, so be it.* You'd think he was the godfather of the Mafia or something, instead of a nerdy kid trying to win the science fair. *Once healed, I shall be back on track with a much bigger and much more important project!*

Darn. For a minute there, I thought the Bunsen burner was on *my* team.

$$\ast\ast\ast$$

Marilee was obviously willing to talk to me about Henry, but not Peterson's Mountain. After lying on my bed for two more hours and staring at the light fixture on my ceiling, I'd had it. I hoped the horse would whinny so loud that Marilee's bedroom windows would rattle.

AllagashRobbie: NEVER MIND ABOUT HENRY!

AllagashRobbie: I WANT TO TALK AND I WANT TO TALK NOW! AND YOU KNOW ABOUT WHAT!!

The rooster sounded almost scared when it crowed.

MeMarilee: Be right over.

When she arrived, Marilee sat on the end of my bed, wearing her black Nikes instead of those ugly red sneakers.

"What do you want me to say?" she asked. She looked pale.

"Only the truth," I answered.

"Okay, I saw a big, big ship of some kind. It was huge. It had lights under it. It chased Johnny. The light that shone in the cave wasn't a four-wheeler. It had to be that thing in the sky. We lost two hours of time. Satisfied?"

"Finally," I said, and let out a sigh of relief.

"I think this calls for an ice cream," said Marilee.

Marilee and I have a philosophy about ice cream. It's good for the brain. We might even have our brains preserved after we die and then donated to science. But we'll only sign the papers if our brains are frozen in ice cream.

✱✱✱

At Flagg's Grocery we ran into two girls from our class, Lydia and Sydni. The four of us bought our ice creams and were sitting next to our bikes on the grassy hill by the library when we heard a siren in the distance. The thing about a siren in a small town like ours is that it gets your attention right away. In the city, I figure people hear sirens all day long and don't pay any attention since there are hundreds of thousands, even millions, of people there. But in a town like Allagash, a siren means that someone you know is in trouble.

Sometimes, although it's rare, they're in trouble with the law and that siren is blue and on the top of a police car. But most of the time it's red and on the top of an ambulance. And it's coming to pick up a neighbor or a family member. So it's a scary sound until the ambulance stops at someone's house or at the nursing home, and then telephones ring all over town and you finally have an answer as to who it's for. We watched in awed silence as the red light flew past us and disappeared around the corner at Flagg's Grocery.

"I bet it's for Mr. Kingsland," Lydia said. "Mom said the hospital sent him home too soon, especially since it's pneumonia he has and he's almost ninety."

"Or it could be for Della's mother," said Sydney. "She's been sick for some time now."

"Or maybe Joey Wallace made another fake phone call," said Marilee. It was known all over town that Joey would get bored now and then and start phoning up places he shouldn't. Sometimes he would call Flagg's Grocery store and ask the owner if he had pigs' feet. When Bill Flagg said yes, that he did indeed have them, Joey would shout, "Well, put on shoes and no one will ever know it!"

"Maybe Freddy jumped off his dad's barn again," I said. "Or the schoolhouse roof." Joey Wallace had once bet Freddy Goble a dollar that he didn't dare jump off his father's barn. Freddy *did* dare and he broke an ankle in doing so. But he got his dollar before he limped into the back of the ambulance, which had been called since Freddy also knocked himself out when he hit the ground and people weren't sure for a time if he was still alive. Just as the ambulance was pulling up next to the barn, Freddy sat up and asked for his dollar.

Then Joey gave him five dollars to jump off the school building, which was a lot higher than the barn. Freddy broke both ankles in that jump and also cracked his funny bone, which wasn't funny at all, especially to his mother. But, businessman that he was, Freddy made four more dollars than with the barn jump. So when we heard the ambulance, we always hoped that it might be Joey Wallace or Freddy Goble behind it. That meant no one was sick or dying, unless it might be Freddy jumping from the bridge or parachuting out of an airplane.

We were just finishing our ice cream cones when the ambulance came roaring back down the road, headed to the hospital in Fort Kent. When an ambulance goes by, I always feel like maybe I should put my hand across my heart or something, the way folks here do when a hearse goes by with a dearly beloved. And this time, I *really* felt that way and I wasn't sure why. I noticed the outline of a person in the back, leaning over what was probably a patient on a stretcher. Something seemed familiar about that silhouette. But I figured it might be Freddy's mom and maybe he'd broken both his legs this time. Possibly even his neck.

I was wrong. Dead wrong. But I didn't know that as Johnny biked by and I decided to follow my brother home. I said, "See ya later," to Marilee and Sydni and Lydia as I got back on my bike and kicked up my stand.

Funny how just the sound of a siren can change your life forever.

15
OUR GREAT LOSS

I was just biking into my front yard, following Johnny's rear bumper, when it hit me who that silhouette looked like. I got a sick feeling in my stomach, but I was still telling myself it was just a feeling, not a fact. But then I saw Mom standing on the front porch waiting for us, and I knew it wasn't just a feeling anymore. Her face was the kind of white I rarely saw, the color human beings keep for the real big and sad stuff that life has to offer. Deathly white. She had a hand up to her mouth. Her other hand held the remote phone to her ear. Then she lowered the phone and looked at us, her eyes shiny with big tears.

"Your grandpa just had a heart attack," she said. It was *Grandma's* silhouette I saw in the ambulance. I knew it. "Uncle Horace is driving up from Bangor as fast as he can.

Marilee's mom has taken your sister over to her house. You kids stay here and wait until Daddy gets home."

And then, before we could even beg to go with her and just sit in the waiting room, as if maybe we could help by being there, she went running toward her car. It backed out of our drive and up onto the road. Mom gave us one last quick look, as if to say she loved us and please stay safe until she got back from the hospital. And then she sped off down the road.

✳✳✳

Johnny and I had microwaved a pizza, which was my specialty since how many science geeks do you know who are great cooks? And we had eaten it while we watched *Top Gear*, which is his favorite show about cars, and I sort of like it too. But nothing could take our minds off Grandpa and what might be going on at the hospital. I imagined him getting up from the bed, smiling and happy, and saying stuff like maybe Loring Air Force Base was behind them making him wear a hospital gown and stuff like that. I thought if I pictured him being well and happy, maybe he would be. But then Dad drove in the yard really fast and we heard his door slam. By the time he came in the front door, he was pretending he was all calm and that he hadn't driven fast at all. We both knew he was putting on a face for us so we wouldn't get upset. A kid can tell a lot from what parents *don't* say.

"Your mom wants to know if you'd like to come and visit your grandpa," he said, his voice soft and steady. I almost got excited about seeing my grandfather, but I could tell by Dad's eyes that it wasn't good. Johnny grabbed his jacket and I grabbed my sweater.

✳ ✳ ✳

Mom was in the waiting room, peering up at the clock when we got there. She smiled at me, a sad smile, as she wrapped her arms around me and squeezed me tight. Then she did the same to Johnny. There was a peace about her now, as if she had accepted whatever was to come.

"Your grandpa is probably not going to make it," she said. She pushed hair behind both of my ears, and ordinarily I'd have told her, "Mom, pleeeeezzze don't do that.

You know how I hate it!" But I said nothing. Let her push all the hair she wanted to. She wasn't even aware that she was doing it anyway. "But I have a feeling he can hear us. And I knew you two would want to say good-bye."

I felt my head nodding and then my dad took my hand just as if I were still a little girl. That was okay too, because I felt like a baby just then. I needed my father and my mother and my big brother. We followed Mom down the long hallway, passing rooms where faces peered out at us. When we reached a door that said No Visitors, she looked back at Johnny and me.

"Ready?" she asked.

"We're ready, Mom," Johnny said, and I was glad because I really didn't feel like talking, even if I could. Mom opened the door, and Johnny, Dad, and I followed her into Grandpa's room. I saw Grandma sitting at the bedside, her hand holding her husband's hand. When she saw us, she smiled as if she really meant it.

Johnny went first to Grandpa and reached for his other hand. I saw a tube in Grandpa's nose, giving him oxygen, I guess. He was hooked up to an IV as well. His hair looked more gray in that room, as if maybe he had aged in the time it had taken the ambulance to get him to the emergency room. Usually, when he was sitting in our backyard by the fireplace, he looked almost as young as my dad. Well, not really, but I wanted to think thoughts right then that would make Grandpa happy.

"It's me, Grandpa," my brother said. "It's Johnny." He squeezed Grandpa's hand and then stepped back for me to take my turn. My knees felt all rubbery, but I stepped forward and reached for my grandfather's hand. It felt too cold for a hand to feel in the summertime, even in an air-conditioned room. I wanted to say something smart-alecky, knowing it would make him smile. But somehow I just couldn't find it in my heart right then to say, "So, any pretty nurses around here? Better not let Grandma find out."

Instead, I squeezed his hand tight and then leaned close and whispered in his ear. "Grandpa?" I said, so softly no one else could hear me. "It's me. Your favorite blond granddaughter. Thank you for showing me the robin's nest. I'll never forget it."

"I think his eyelids just moved," I heard Mom say. I hope she was right, and that my grandfather heard me. It was our little joke since I'm his *only* blond granddaughter. Tina is dark-haired, like our dad. So at least I put some humor into saying good-bye, especially since I got my sense of humor from him. Everyone always said so.

We sat in the waiting room then, Johnny and Dad and I, since Mom thought it would be best for us. Uncle Horace finally arrived, having driven up from Bangor where he'd gone on business. Aunt Betty was with him. They disappeared down the hall and into Grandpa's room. That was at 4:45 p.m.

At 7:34 p.m., Mom and Grandma came into the waiting room to find us. Grandma had a handkerchief and was blowing her nose. Her eyes were red and swollen. Mom looked as pale as ever. But she smiled at us again, and I knew she would come and hug us tight and tell us how much she loved us. And that Grandpa had loved us too, but that now he was gone. And that's just what she did.

✳ ✳ ✳

On the morning of the funeral, three days later, I got on my bike and went riding down the path that led to

Frog Pond. I leaned my bike against a birch tree and then walked in under the leaves and branches. On weekends, Grandpa always cut our firewood for winter there, rock maple and birch and poplar. When he was working, I'd sometimes bring him a thermos of hot tea. Then we'd sit and talk about anything and everything.

"Cut your wood in the spring, and it'll season well enough for autumn and winter," Grandpa said. "Rock maple burns longest." It was just that spring while we were having our tea that he showed me the robin's nest. It was wedged into the branch of a poplar. "Robins have been building a nest there every year that I've been cutting my firewood here," Grandpa said. "You watch, Robbie. Any day now, that nest will have sky-blue eggs and then babies."

I counted five baby birds, their red mouths open and begging their mama for food, before I biked back home and put on a dress for Grandpa's funeral.

★ ★ ★

Grandpa Bob's funeral was one of the biggest ones Allagash had ever seen. It took Harold Hopkins, our temporary sheriff, and two men he had deputized just to direct the traffic out to Woodlawn Acres, the biggest of the three small cemeteries in Allagash. Johnny and I rode with Grandma and my parents in the car behind the hearse. Uncle Horace and Aunt Betty followed in their own car. I tried to imagine the jokes Grandpa would be telling, such as, "Well, I always knew I'd own a long, black, fancy car one day." Thinking of him that way gave me some comfort, even if I knew he was never coming back. Grandma was being *brave for the children*, or so I heard her telling my mother before the service at the church. Mom was doing the same.

"I never saw so many flowers before inside that church," Grandma said as Mom squeezed her hand. "Bob would be so proud of that."

"He had a lot of good friends," said my father.

The hearse put on its blinker and then just sat there in the middle of the road, blinking. Cars pulled up behind us and stopped. Everyone was too polite, given the event, to do any honking. So we waited, wondering what was happening that the procession had come to a halt. Then we saw two skinny hands waving like flags in front of the gate to the cemetery.

"Oh, for heaven's sake," said Grandma. "That poor simpleton Harold Hopkins is trying to direct traffic with the sense God gave a goose."

"He probably doesn't know his left from his right," said my dad.

And then we were all laughing and saying how it sounded just like the things Grandpa might say. It was a nice way to say good-bye. Finally, when Harold Hopkins figured out which was left and which was right, the hearse started moving again and soon pulled up alongside the grave site. Our car parked next to it. My dad got out and helped Grandma and my mom out. Then Johnny and I followed. We met up with Uncle Horace and Aunt Betty, and as a family unit we stood and listened to the minister talk about my grandfather's good life. Grandma threw some gravel onto the top of his coffin as it was being lowered. Then the rest of us did the same.

My grandfather, Robert Allen Carter, disappeared from our lives that day.

16
MENDING OUR HEARTS

After Grandpa's death, life seemed dreamlike for a time, slow motion, as if we were living underwater. I put all plans to contact aliens aside since my heart just wasn't in it. Mom said we wouldn't have any more cookouts that summer at the backyard fireplace, since it would only make Grandma sad. Instead, we found a huge rock by the river and Dad brought it to our backyard in his pickup truck. We all took our turns writing messages on it to Grandpa. Even Grandma did it. It was like a little memorial in our backyard. I was the last one to take the Magic Marker. *All the baby robins have flown from the nest, Grandpa*, I wrote. It was true. I had walked down to count them just that morning.

Marilee continued to call and e-mail and instant message and just be a soft shoulder when I needed one to cry on. But I think she was grateful that I'd stopped talking about contacting aliens. And then, I'd grown up a lot in just the past month. Loss can do that to a person. For me, it was getting up at night to go to the bathroom and hearing my mom crying in her bedroom. Or seeing Grandma's sad face when her own birthday came, even though we took her to the River Café for the all-you-can-eat breakfast and Darlene brought out a cupcake with a big candle on it. Or seeing Uncle Horace sit alone to watch the Boston Red Sox, instead of next to Grandpa on the sofa, both of them wearing caps with a big red B, for Boston. Those were the things that hurt *me* the most, even though I missed Grandpa too.

On a sunny day, a month after Grandpa died, I decided to go visit his grave and also check on the geranium I'd given Mom to plant for me. I hoped it had made it through the last big thunderstorm. The seeds the funeral home planted had sprouted well, and now the grass was thick and green on his grave. And the geranium was all pink blossoms. I noticed other flowers and plants near the headstone and assumed Grandma and Mom had put them there. I didn't have to wonder who had left the

Boston Red Sox cap. It had been pushed inside a plastic freezer bag and then placed next to my geranium.

As I was snipping dead leaves from the plants, I noticed a man standing in front of a tombstone near the back fence. When he saw me, he waved and I waved back.

"How are things going, young lady?" he asked.

It was Mr. Mallory, our former sheriff. I stood and brushed the dirt from my jeans. Then I said a quick good-bye to Grandpa, with a promise to visit him again the next week. I made my way past other headstones, pausing now and then to pay my respects when it was someone I remembered, such as Mrs. Ethel O'Leary. Mrs. O'Leary had been my babysitter from the time I was born until I got old enough to stay home on my own.

"Hello, Mr. Mallory," I said. "I guess things are going okay," I added, finally answering his question. I looked at the writing on the stone he was visiting. *Simon Joseph Mallory. 1930–2001*.

"You probably don't remember my father," he said, and nodded at the name.

"No, sir," I said. "But I heard of him. Grandpa used to say he was a very fine lawman."

"He was," Mr. Mallory said, his eyes looking sad. "He was, and he taught me everything I know."

"Why do people have to die?" I was surprised I asked this. But it just sort of popped out. I mean, I sort of know the answer. It's all a part of the Great Plan, whatever that is.

"Well," said Mr. Mallory. "That's a tough one. And there are all kinds of answers to it. As many answers as there are religions in the world. And for those folks who don't believe in a religion or a god, I guess their answer would be that it's just nature's way."

"It's a stupid way," I said, "no matter how you answer it."

"I couldn't agree with you more," he said. "But all we can do while we're on the planet, Roberta, is our very best. My dad used to say we should leave Earth better off than when we found it. If we can do that, then we've done our part."

"How can we leave it better?" I asked. "By recycling maybe?" I needed to get that Coke bottle out of the trash and put it in Mom's recycling barrel. What was I thinking by throwing it away?

"That's one way, for sure," said our former sheriff, although it was still hard for me to think of him that way, especially now that Harold Hopkins seemed likely to become his replacement at the next town elections.

"Do you still miss your dad?" I asked. I was hoping someone would tell me that one day the sadness would go away.

"I do," he said, "and I think of him every day. But our job as those left behind is to live and enjoy ourselves while we're here. Your grandpa would want you to do that, Roberta."

"Grandpa told me not to spit into the wind," I said then. "He told me to always keep the wind at my back."

"Well, that's certainly good advice," Mr. Mallory said. "Bob Carter was a fine man."

"Grandpa was always giving me advice," I said. It was true. *Never give the devil a ride 'cause he'll want to drive. Don't change horses in the middle of the stream. A whistling girl and a crowing hen always come to a bad end.* Although, I have to admit I never understood that last one.

"My father gave me good advice too," Mr. Mallory said then. We both watched as a rabbit scooted out from behind a headstone and began munching the clover that grew nearby. "He always said, 'To thine own self be true.'

That's pretty good counsel." I kicked the end of my Nike at a red plastic rose that had blown off one of the floral pieces and watched it roll a few inches and stop.

"Yup, Sheriff, I reckon it is and that's a dang fact," I said. I don't really talk like that. I mean, I've never said the words "reckon" or "dang" in my life. But I had just watched an old black-and-white Western with Dad. In one scene, a cowboy pushes his hat back on his head and says that to the town sheriff. Then he kicks a tumbleweed with his boot. I thought it was the coolest line. And when was the last time you kicked a tumbleweed, which is really a hedgehog with no legs?

"Yup, I reckon it is," I said again and kicked the plastic rose once more. I saw a slight smile play around Mr. Mallory's mouth.

"Well, I better be getting on home," he said. "Mrs. Mallory has probably called Harold Hopkins by now and reported me missing."

"I wouldn't worry about him finding you," I said. "Not unless you stop at the River Café for a donut."

Mr. Mallory smiled outwardly this time. But before he left, he looked again at his father's grave. Beneath the name and the date were these words that we read together silently: *Lord, who may dwell in your sanctuary? Who may live on your holy hill? He whose walk is blameless and who does what is righteous, and who speaks the truth from his heart. —Psalm 15:1–2.*

"Now, that's a dang fact, Sheriff," I said, when I'd finished reading.

✳ ✳ ✳

About 3 p.m., while Stanley Mallory and I were visiting the cemetery, something interesting happened out on Highway 42, right at the turnoff to the Tom Leonard farm. Our mailman, Larry Fitz, saw a red jeep pulled off to the side of the road. A baseball cap lay near the front tire. It was Joey Wallace's jeep, the only red jeep in Allagash. It was his favorite cap, the one with a fly hook pinned just above the words "Gone Fishing." The keys were still in the ignition, but there was no sign of Joey. Word of this went around town in minutes. Had anyone seen Joey Wallace? It was finally determined that he was last seen buying a hot dog and an orange pop at Cramer's

Gas & Movie Rentals. Then, he'd driven off in the direction of Highway 42.

That Joey Wallace was our local clown didn't help matters, since almost everyone believed it was another of his foolish pranks. "Crazy Joey Wallace" is what Grandma had called him when he asked Sheriff Mallory if he'd been drinking beer that day of the press conference. Joey once took a sheet of white cardboard, four feet long and two feet wide. On the front, he drew a perfect check and made it out for a million dollars. Then he stuck on a fake mustache, put on a pair of eyeglasses, and dressed in a suit. He knocked on Mrs. Barton's front door and pretended to be the man from Publishers Clearing House. It took her neighbors twenty minutes to calm Phyllis Barton down long enough to tell her that she *hadn't* won a million dollars.

Another time, during a full moon, Joey climbed to the top of the Allagash water tower and spent the entire night up there on the walkway near the top. When we asked why he did it, he said, "I wanted to get a closer look at the moon."

A month or two rarely passed without Joey Wallace

playing some stupid trick on someone. So, while folks were concerned, everyone felt pretty sure that Joey was hiding out someplace, probably near a telephone so he could make crank calls. We figured he wanted us to think aliens had taken him. That would top all of his other jokes and maybe get him national attention, which he craved.

Whether Joey was joking or not was really none of my business. I was still disappointed in my fellow man, considering most of them were ostriches. But, mainly, I was brokenhearted over losing my grandfather.

17
MORE BREAKING NEWS

The next day, when I got home from returning a book to the library, Marilee was sitting on my front steps. She followed me up the stairs to my bedroom and waited until I closed the door on any ears within hearing distance.

"I've been thinking," she said. "It's time we got focused again with our science project. Those aliens aren't going to sit up there and wait forever."

"What?" I asked. I figured my ears had filled up with wind and dust as I biked back from the library. "Is this the Gutless Wonder I see before me?"

"Henry has a new project," Marilee said. "I heard him telling his mother on their back porch. His bandages are off now and he's back in action."

"What's his project?" I asked, my heart wondering if it should beat calmly or wildly.

"He's crossing a hollyhock with a burdock," said Marilee. "He's calling it 'the Helmsby Hollydock.'"

"But what's the point in even *doing* that?" I asked.

"It's something about how the flower will then have prickly needles protecting it so that bees can't steal the pollen," she said. I thought about this. It sounded like it might or should be important to mankind, but I still didn't see how.

"When was the last time a hollyhock filed a burglary charge on a bee?" I asked, and Marilee laughed out loud. I mean, bees need pollen to eat. But mostly, they carry pollen from one flower to another to fertilize them. Did Henry think the world had too many hollyhocks, one of our prettiest flowers? Okay, this might be the best time to tell you about Henry Helmsby and the Barbie dolls.

It all started when Henry decided he could improve upon Barbie's hair. He had put strands from his sister Pearl's doll under his microscope and saw that they were made of synthetic fibers. So Henry wondered if plant fibers such as bamboo might also work. If so, it might save the Mattel toy company something like fifty cents a year. They would get all excited and want to buy his research. As I said, Henry is a science geek. He's not an accountant. He did some figuring with a pencil and decided that he needed twenty-five Barbie dolls to conduct his work.

A Barbie doll isn't cheap, but Henry's father is. Henry's weekly allowance of three dollars meant he could buy one Barbie every two months if didn't spend a penny on anything else. He soon realized that he'd be in high school by the time he could even begin his research. Therefore, Barbie dolls started disappearing all over town.

Shawna O'Neal had left three of hers lying on a picnic blanket in the school park. When she returned from getting a soda pop, all three were gone. Lexi Desjardins had put hers in her mom's shopping cart while she inspected the potato chips at Flagg's Grocery. Same thing. Gone. Caitlin Overlock left two Barbies sitting on her porch steps discussing their wardrobes while she went inside to answer the phone. No sign of the Barbies when she returned.

Over and over again, everywhere in town, little girls were losing their Barbie dolls and calling Sheriff Mallory and bursting into loud tears. After the sheriff's ears couldn't take the crying anymore, he decided to let

Deputy Harold Hopkins do a stakeout with his grand-daughter's Barbie. He figured Harold would be able to handle a doll caper. The stakeout Barbie was dressed in a snappy red sweater and a blue denim skirt and was placed strategically near the drop box at the post office. Deputy Hopkins sat hidden behind the oak tree across the road and ate a box of chocolate donuts as he waited.

Sure enough, in no time Henry Helmsby was observed crawling, crab-like, out from behind the mailboxes at the side of the post office. He snatched up Barbie and ran, the deputy right behind him with the blue light swirling and the siren roaring on the police car. Sheriff Mallory wasn't happy that Harold had made the arrest of a boy over a Barbie doll so public. It wasn't really an arrest anyway, since the sheriff just drove Henry over to his house and talked quietly to his parents.

Mr. Helmsby found a box up in Henry's room with twenty bald Barbies all reaching their arms up, as if plead-ing for help. Henry was forced to mow lawns all that summer to pay for the dolls that Mrs. Helmsby drove to Caribou to buy and replace. When Pearl Helmsby got her new doll, she kept it under lock and key in her bedroom. The kids at school figured Barbie might just pack her suitcase one night, throw it into the trunk of her pink Corvette, and drive away from Allagash, rather than live in the same house with Henry.

"Are you even listening to me?" Marilee was asking and waving a hand in front of my face.

"Sorry," I said, and shook the cobwebs from my mind. "I was thinking of Henry."

"I'm really not here about Henry," she said. "I know you've had the heart kicked out of you lately. I mean, I still have both my grandfathers. So it's time your best friend took charge for a while."

Somebody get the smelling salts—and get a lot of them. But I knew she was just saying this stuff to cheer me up. All I had to do was call her bluff. And once I got my heart back, that's just what I would do.

"What do you think happened to Joey Wallace?" she asked then. The whole town was humming about his disappearance. You could almost hear it too, like the noise you make when you rub a wet finger around the mouth of a glass.

"I don't think aliens would take Joey," I told her. "If

they did, they'd know in thirty seconds it was a mistake and put him back."

"Then where is he?" Marilee asked.

"Uncle Horace says Joey has a girlfriend down in Caribou. He says that's who abducted him. He's probably hoping this will get big enough for the story to go viral."

"Girls?" Mom was shouting up the stairs, a habit of hers lately. "You should come down and hear this."

***

In the living room, Mom had the TV on. I could see Stanley Mallory's face. They had interrupted the local news, Mom said, for an important message.

"I had hoped this UFO thing would quiet down so we could live in peace," said Mom. "I don't think the White House has this many press conferences in a month."

After a few blasts of feedback from the microphone, Stanley Mallory cleared his throat and looked directly into the camera.

"Folks, I've had a lot of sleepless nights in the past month," he said. "I've been tossing and turning over what is right and what is wrong. Yesterday, I paid a visit to someone I haven't talked to in a long time, someone who always gave me good advice along with the cold, hard truth."

"'Lord, who may dwell in your sanctuary?'" I recited. "'Who may live on your holy hill?'"

"What?" asked Mom.

"What?" asked Marilee.

"Nothing," I said, my eyes still glued to the television.

"Now I stand here before you today," Mr. Mallory continued, "ashamed to admit that I lied to you all. I also want to thank a young citizen of this town for helping me make this decision I'm about to announce."

When Mom glanced suspiciously at me, I shrugged my shoulders. But I could feel my heart coming back to me. I could feel my old self rising up and wanting to enjoy my life again as Grandpa would want me to, just as Stanley Mallory had said.

"I saw something that night on Highway 42 that I couldn't identify or explain," he was saying now. "That means it was a UFO. More than that, I doubt it's a craft of the planet Earth. It was eons ahead of any technology we have here. I should have stuck to my story, since it was the truth. Now, someone from this town is missing.

"I'm not saying Joey Wallace was abducted. You all know Joey and how he loves a good joke. But I should have done my job to protect him and all of you. I didn't. Now, I don't care if this makes the mayor unhappy and the entire Chamber of Commerce. The truth is the truth."

Tons of questions flew at him, but he refused them. He held up a hand for silence.

"And what's more, I am withdrawing my resignation as sheriff. I have a missing person report to deal with. If you folks no longer want me in this job, then you can vote me out at the next town meeting."

Cheers flooded the room. Faces were smiling and hands clapping, everyone but poor Harold Hopkins, who would be just a deputy again. Even the journalists stopped writing to applaud. Mom turned off the television.

"Where did you go yesterday on your bike?" she asked.

I would have answered her, but I was already out the door, Marilee behind me. We stopped on the front porch and looked at each other.

"Oh, my gosh," Marilee said. "They really exist, don't they?"

"Marilee," I said. "We have less than a month before school starts again." It was true. It felt as if the summer had rolled up like a caterpillar and just disappeared on us. "We can think up a new project, but why switch horses in midstream?"

"I guess you're right," Marilee said.

"Of course, I'm right," I said. "Otherwise, we're spitting into the wind."

"I suppose."

"We can't let Henry Helmsby win," I said. I was on a roll. My heart felt good to be talking again and now it wouldn't shut up. "If we do, that's like giving the devil a ride and letting him drive."

"Hmmm," said Marilee, and I knew she was thinking about the devil driving a car.

"And remember," I said, "a whistling girl and a crowing hen always come to a bad end."

"Huh?"

"I've got a plan," I said. "I worked on it the whole time you were grounded, and also while you had your head in the sand. I put it aside when Grandpa died. But now I'm taking it off the back burner and putting it right on that big burner at the front of the stove. It makes anything I ever planned before in my life look like kindergarten."

"No!" said Marilee, shaking her head. You could understand her hesitation about ingenious plans, I suppose. After all, *she* was the one living next door to the Helmsbys when their greenhouse blew up.

"Just hear me out before you say no," I pleaded. "Let's go lie on our rocks by the river and discuss it."

"Didn't you just hear me say no, Robbie?"

"It's gonna be big, Marilee. Humongous. Right up there alongside the discovery of fire and the invention of the wheel. Trust me."

"*No!*"

But she crawled on behind me as I put the four-wheeler in gear.

18
The Grand Scheme

J ust listen to it, okay?" We were lying on our rocks, watching the clouds float by. Hearing Sheriff Mallory admit what I knew to be true had fueled me. "I'm not talking *state* science fair now. I may not even be talking national. This would be so big, Marilee, that it could very well be international."

"Okay, let's hear it," she said. "But I know I won't like it and that my answer will be no. After falling into that well on Peterson's Mountain, we're lucky to be alive."

"*We* go after *them*," I said. "We contact them and we become the second generation of Allagash Abductions. There will probably be a movie made. Katy Perry could play you, and Taylor Swift could play me."

"Are you insane? Besides, they're too old."

"I'm not insane, I'm brilliant. We contact the aliens by

signaling from the mouth of Peterson's Cave. They tend to show up in the same places. I read all about this while you were hiding out, avoiding the subject."

"How would this qualify for a science fair?"

"The whole idea of the competition is that we explore the wonders of science and open up our possibilities. I'd say going aboard a spacecraft is that times a million."

"*No*, and it's a 'no' the size of that spaceship we saw. Double the size."

"We'll be more than famous, Marilee," I said. "We'll be the first kids to stage and then record an actual abduction. We'll be like space detectives."

"Sure. And how many space detectives do you know?"

"None."

"Right. That's 'cause they're all dead."

"Or better yet, Marilee," I said, "what would you think of becoming a UFO chaser? We'd be the only two girls in history. I'll build us a website. I can go to Photoshop and make us some cool badges, shiny ones like Harold Hopkins has."

"And how do we record an abduction?"

"We take a camera with us. I'll hide it in my jacket pocket."

"Oh, please. They fly across galaxies, Robbie. You think they wouldn't find a camera?"

"Okay, but we get taken aboard," I said. "*Again*, may I add, since there's no doubt they've already taken us once."

"Then why would they want us again? They put us back, remember?"

"You got it backward. *We* want *them*." I smiled. Sometimes, Marilee can actually seem less bright than she really is.

"And how do we tell them that?"

"We send them alphabet letters that spell words," I said. "They are advanced beyond our imaginations or they wouldn't be able to visit Earth. They wouldn't have those amazing spacecraft. English words or words in any language would be nothing for them to translate. They can pick up the words we send, and in a nanosecond they'll understand our message."

"And how do we send them a message? E-mail or snail mail?"

"Very funny," I said. "This is what we'll use." I pulled my mom's iPhone 4 from my pocket. Mom uses it when she goes shopping to Fort Kent or to visit her sister in

Caribou, places lucky enough to have reception. I put the phone in Marilee's hand. She looked at it and laughed out loud. She even kicked her feet up and down on her rock. Two merganser ducks floating down the river flapped their wings and flew, leaving a trail of water droplets.

"That's the funniest thing I've ever heard!" Marilee squealed, finally able to speak. "We just telephone them! Or do we text message? And then, even on Peterson's Mountain there is no cell phone reception in Allagash! Oh, I'm going to die from laughing! My life is over!"

I had expected this. I really had. I waited patiently until she was sane again.

"This iPhone is also a camera, as you know," I said. "All we need is a Light-O-Matic application for its camera flash and we can use Morse code."

"You don't *know* Morse code, Einstein."

"Maybe not, but the application does." I unfolded the instructions I'd downloaded and printed for the Light-O-Matic app. I had bought it from the iTunes store just after our famous night on the mountain. For the whole week that no one would talk to me about our experience, I had been planning. Thanks to trusty Google—*how to send Morse code signals*—I found out about the Light-O-Matic application for iPhone 4's camera flash. Marilee was reading the instructions. She wasn't laughing now.

"Wow," she said.

"The application gives you a choice of a strobe light, flashlight, or a Morse code translator. I've already installed the translator. All I do is key in my words and the flash will send out the message."

"*Wow!*" said Marilee. She handed the instructions back to me. "But it's getting scary again, Roberta McKinnon. I don't like it one bit."

"If we're abducted *again*, they will put us back *again*. We have nothing to worry about."

"But if we remember nothing, how can we do our project?" Marilee was biting at her fingernail so I knew she was nervous. Nervous, but hooked.

"Maybe we find the same man who hypnotized the Vermont Four," I said. "The man who wrote *The Allagash Abductions*. Did you know he lives in southern Maine?"

"What message will you send them?"

"I don't know," I admitted. I had been playing around with ideas until we lost Grandpa. But I knew I could come up with something perfect. I pulled up a blade of the wild hay that grows near my river rock. "I'm still working on it. It has to be exactly right." I bit down on the hay, tasting its sweetness.

"Oh, I don't like this, I don't like this, I don't like this," Marilee was saying. She got up from the rock and grabbed her towel. "This is one of your genius plans we might not get out of."

I twirled the blade of hay between two fingers.

"I don't think international is too big as far as science fairs go," I said. "But we might have to consider intergalactic."

"Robbie, this is insane."

"I can always do the project alone," I said. "You know, receive all the glory and attention and money for myself. Rather than sharing it with my best friend."

"I have to think about this," said Marilee.

That was all I needed to hear. I knew I had her. I threw the blade of hay and watched it hit the water. It swirled around and around in a fast current. Helpless, it was soon carried off downstream. I guess you could say it was caught up in circumstances it had no control over. You might say it *imploded.* I sometimes wondered if that's how Marilee Evans felt, just being my friend.

19
CRYING WOLF

WE COME IN PEACE.

TAKE US TO YOUR LEADER.

BEAM US UP, SCOTTY.

HOW'S THE WEATHER UP THERE?

SEEN ANY GOOD GALAXIES LATELY?

DON'T FORGET TO TAKE OUT THE SPACE TRASH.

WHEN IN DOUBT, GOOGLE.

Okay, we were being silly. Or I was, anyway. But thinking up a perfect message to send by Morse code to aliens isn't as easy as it sounds. It had to say a lot in a few words. Marilee was lying on the bed and looking at my *Star Wars* poster. I was at my computer.

"This will be extra cool since kids are almost never

abducted," I said. I deleted, *BE OUR FRIENDS, PLEASE*, before Marilee could even say it was stupid.

"Maybe it's because they hate kids and that's another reason for us to stay home."

"Who could hate us, Marilee?"

"What if it's a different spaceship that reads the message and not the one we saw the other night? What if they take us and don't put us back? What if they can't understand Morse code? What if they're dyslexic?"

What if, what if, what if. Marilee was driving me crazy.

"Keep it up and I'll go alone," I said.

"Do we pack anything?" She was sitting in the middle of my bed now in a lotus position. She learned yoga in Boston and loves it. She says it keeps her focused, which helps since I'm her best friend and always trying to talk her into something crazy.

"Sure, we take our winter boots, our bicycles, school books, my cat and your dog, my goldfish, and a tuna sandwich. Of course, we don't pack anything! We'll only be gone a couple hours, remember?"

"But if they already examined us, what would they do with us all that time?"

That was a darn good question. So I ignored it.

"We're going to communicate with them," I said. "To learn about them as they learned about us."

"Oh please, that is so much bull," said Marilee. "We're going so we can win at science fair."

"Okay, but they don't know that," I said, and turned off my computer. "Let's go to Cramer's for an ice cream."

I can think better when I'm not trying so hard. I knew the message had to be short and tempting. Like bait on a fishing hook.

"What about 'Justin Bieber rules'?"

"Please. They've never heard of him. He's Canadian."

"*Everyone* has heard of him," said Marilee. "In every galaxy." She flopped back into the position of a human being, instead of a lotus.

The way I looked at it, there was no need to waste time. Maybe they only visit other galaxies in certain seasons, the way the tourists come to Maine's ocean. They might even be gone back to their own galaxy by now. Summer aliens. We had to act fast or fail faster.

"We'll do it tomorrow night," I said to Marilee. It was a hot day and I could almost taste the ice cream.

"So soon?"

"Yes, so it'll be over soon. But just in case, you know, something goes wrong, we need to do the film."

"What film?" she asked.

"I'll tell you tomorrow," I said. "So be at my house after supper, okay? Ask your mom if you can spend the night."

"You mean after *dinner*?" asked Marilee. I sighed.

"About six o'clock, smart aleck. Now let's go get an ice cream."

✱✱✱

After making her promise not to be late tomorrow night, I said good-bye to Marilee and rode back home on my bike. I had an ice cream for Tina and didn't want it to melt. I got off my bike and leaned it against the porch railing. That's when I noticed a blue car in our driveway. Then I heard Mom's voice as she talked to someone in the backyard. I figured she was working in her garden and that Tina would be with her.

It was Mary Wallace's blue car. She was sitting at the cast-iron table with Mom. Tina was driving her Little

Tykes Push & Ride Racer back and forth from the clothesline to the toolshed. As I tore the wrapper from the ice cream, she drove up to my feet and stopped. Then she grabbed the treat with her chubby little hands and bit into its coolness.

"You better put your car in park," I told her. "You don't want Sheriff Mallory to write you a ticket."

"Roberta, come here, please," Mom said.

"Hello, Roberta," said Mrs. Wallace.

"Mary is here because, as you know, her son, Joey, is missing," said Mom, and handed me a flyer with a picture on it. There was Joey's stupid grin, as if he was up to no good again. MISSING! it said above his head. $500 REWARD FOR INFORMATION! it said below. TWENTY-FIVE YEARS OLD. BROWN HAIR AND EYES.

"He wouldn't pull a trick like this on me," Mary was saying now, and her voice quivered a bit. "I've been going all over town putting up these flyers so folks will know it's not a joke."

"I'm sorry, Mrs. Wallace," I said. I had to hand it to Joey. To get your mother to take part in a major prank like this was pretty awesome. His smiling face on the flyer looked like he was almost winking at the world. "I'll be sure to tell everyone I can."

"Thank you, honey," said Mary Wallace.

After the blue car had driven down the road toward Mr. Finley's, I turned to my mom.

"What do you think?" I asked.

"I don't know Mary well," she said. "But I can't imagine any mother being involved in a joke about her missing child. I just can't."

"Do you think Joey is playing this joke on his mother too?"

"Maybe," said Mom. "Joey is like the boy who cried wolf."

"Who's he?"

"It's a fable," she said. "A Greek shepherd boy keeps telling everyone in his village that a wolf is about to attack their sheep. They believe him many times, but there is no wolf. The boy made it up. Then, one day, he really does see a wolf about to attack. He tries to warn people, but they don't believe him. So the wolf kills all the sheep."

"That sucks," I said. "Poor sheep."

"Poor Mary Wallace," said Mom.

20
The Message

I woke up nervous. The entire day passed in a blur. But I was ready and waiting for Marilee when she bounded up the stairs and into my room. She shut the door behind her.

"Lock it," I said, "just in case Johnny comes up."

"Should we put on makeup?" asked Marilee. She was inspecting the camcorder.

"We don't wear makeup, remember? We're too young."

"Child actors wear it."

"It's for our families, Marilee," I said. "Not the Academy Awards show."

"We could put it on YouTube. It might go viral."

"If we don't come back," I said, "you can bet they'll put it on YouTube, and you can bet it'll go viral. It'll be a big news story. I can see Joey Wallace's jealous face now."

I brushed my hair and fixed the collar of my shirt. We didn't need makeup, but we should still look neat. Otherwise, why would anyone search for us? Marilee brushed her own hair. I turned the camera on and checked the zoom lens.

"Okay, sit on the bed and once I get it started, I'll sit next to you."

With the camcorder perched on my desk and aimed at Marilee's head, I hurried over to sit next to her. I put an arm around her shoulder and she did the same to me. I imagined what we would look like if someone saw the video. Two girls, one with long blond hair and one with shorter brown hair, ready for the biggest adventure of their lives. But if everything went as planned, no one would ever see the clip but us. I stared at the red light.

"This is Roberta Angela McKinnon," I said. "I'm eleven years old until I turn twelve in two months. This is my best friend, Marilee Julia Evans. She's also eleven until December. We have a message to leave for our families." I looked over at Marilee. "Do you want to say something too?" I asked.

Marilee smiled at the camcorder. "I'm hungry," she said.

Shoot! I got off the bed and grabbed the camera. I rewound the footage and started over.

"No joking, Marilee," I said. "If it comes down to our parents watching this, that means we're missing."

"Sorry," said Marilee. Her stomach growled right on cue. "But we need to bring some food."

We got situated again, and again I did the introductions.

"If you're watching this," I said, "we're probably missing. We're leaving in a few minutes for Peterson's Cave. Our mission is to signal the spaceship we believe abducted us there and then put us back two hours later. Ask Johnny and Billy about it. Make them tell you the truth. We want to contact the beings aboard that craft to make friends with them and then describe everything that happened for our science project. If we don't return, we know that you'll find this message, Mom, when you come to wake me up tomorrow morning. If that's the case, I'm truly sorry. So is Marilee. Aren't you?" I nudged Marilee.

"I'm sorry, Mom and Dad," said Marilee. "And Sarah."

"You will at least know what happened to us. We promise that we'll do everything we can to return to you. We're famous for getting out of messes, right?" I smiled at this, knowing that Mom would be hysterical by this time, and Dad too. Maybe a little joke would cheer them up. "If we're not here, you will probably find our bikes near Peterson's Cave."

"Unless they take our bikes too," said Marilee. She said this to me, not to the camera.

"Are you crazy?" I said back to Marilee, forgetting the camera. "Why would extraterrestrials want bicycles?"

"If they take us to their planet," said Marilee, "we'll need something to ride. You know, so we can get around."

"You're insane," I said. "They'd give us supersonic boots. Or little cars that fly. Something cool like that."

Marilee was nudging me in the side.

"What?"

"The camcorder," she whispered.

I looked at the camera. No time to record it again. And besides, I didn't think for one second anyone would see it but the two of us. We'd be back by midnight and erase the film before breakfast in the morning.

"I love you, everyone," I said. "Mom. Dad. Johnny. Tina. Grandma. Uncle Horace. Aunt Betty. Sheriff Mallory. All of Allagash."

"Me too," said Marilee. "I love you all."

"Good-bye, Billy," I added.

"Good-bye, Johnny," said Marilee, which I found strange. But I figured she was still thankful that my brother had tried to save us that night on the mountain.

✻ ✻ ✻

At nine, right on cue, I heard Mom and Dad getting ready for bed. First Dad snapped out the porch light and then Mom shut off the television. Their bedroom is on the first floor, an architectural fact that made Johnny and me very happy. Rarely did we hear, "Turn that noise down!" once our parents fell asleep.

"We wait thirty minutes," I said to Marilee. "Make sure they're sleeping." We were both dressed and ready. The flash drive was lying on my pillow on top of a sheet of typing paper with the words: IF WE ARE MISSING, PLEASE WATCH! I had Mom's iPhone in my pocket. The message I wanted to send was still in my head, ready to key into the Morse code translator. It had come to me as I was having breakfast. Two simple words.

At nine thirty, I opened my bedroom door. I could hear a baseball game blasting in Johnny's room and knew he wouldn't hear anything unless a foul ball hit him in the head.

"Follow me," I whispered to Marilee. "Remember to tiptoe."

Downstairs, we slipped out into the yard, past the lilac bush and over to where our bikes were leaning against the toolshed. No way could we take the four-wheeler. We'd wake up the whole house if we did, and maybe all the ghosts on Peterson's Mountain. The moon was now full and the backyard had turned to silver. I watched as Marilee slid a leg over the seat of her bike, and then I did the same to mine. We pedaled slowly out of the driveway, a few creaks that no one would hear.

The meadow was silver too, and the frogs so noisy it sounded like a party was going on at their pond. We glided past and hit the recreation trail that carried us around to the foot of Peterson's Mountain. The cave was only a third of the way up. We could walk our bikes there and use our headlights coming back down. *If* we came back down.

The moonlight was so bright that we almost didn't need headlights. Marilee got off her bike and began pushing it, so I did the same. Off in the distance a screech owl let loose a cry. I felt hair rise on the back of my neck. If you haven't heard a screech owl before, let me tell you that it sounds like the whinny of a ghost horse.

"Maybe we should forget about this," Marilee said. I knew the owl had frightened her. "If we back out, no one would know but us."

"And that's two too many," I said. I took the lead, pushing my bike in front of hers. That's when we heard the haunting fiddle music.

"What's *that*?"

"It's a ghost fiddler."

"Stop it, Robbie! What is it?"

"It's a dead tree," I told her. "The wind is moving it like a fiddle bow across another tree. There's the cave."

★★★

The full moon hung over the Allagash Valley like a silver dollar, sparkling and bright. The night was alive with expectation. We could see fireflies burning up the hayfields down by the river. Half of the lights in town were already out since most country people go to bed early. The gas station was still lit up and so was the police department. Houses here and there had yellow dots of light for windows. I assumed kids my age were watching TV or playing computer games. We leaned our bikes against the cave wall. I took the flashlight out of my backpack and put it on the ground where I could find it later. Marilee was quiet.

"I'll be glad when this night is over," she said.

"Me too." I realized I meant it. So why was I doing it? Well, why did Columbus get on a creaky ship and talk two more creaky ships into following him halfway around the globe? Why did explorers freeze to death at the North Pole? Why did Amelia Earhart try to fly around the world? Why did Neil Armstrong walk on the moon? Why does Paris Hilton dress her dog up in clothes?

I really don't know why I do the things I do. Mom says I have the "wild gene" and that I didn't get it from her side of the family. But everyone in Dad's family seems normal. I guess this is just the way I was born.

"Rub some of this on your face and neck," I said, and handed Marilee the bug repellent.

"Gross," she said. "No way." But a mosquito was buzzing close by, so she changed her mind. "I just thought of something, Robbie. If the aliens look like bugs, we have repellent!"

"Silly," I said.

I got out the iPhone and clicked it on.

"You think the message will work?"

"I hope so," I said.

We heard a coyote howl from the top of the mountain, and I prayed a rabbit wasn't going to die. Dad says the coyote has to live too, but it's still sad. Marilee pulled her sweater tighter about her arms and watched me.

"Remember that spaceship episode of *Twilight Zone*?" she asked.

Marilee and I love watching old *Star Trek* reruns and *Battlestar Galactica*. Maybe it's because we like science. We're girls who want to "boldly go where no man has gone before." *Twilight Zone* episodes were scarier but still fun. I remembered the episode.

"'To Serve Man,'" I said. But I didn't want to think about it.

"The Kanamits," said Marilee. "Nine-foot-tall aliens who ate human beings for dinner."

"Supper," I said. "Don't think of that. Think about us winning the biggest science fair on earth and becoming rich and famous."

I keyed the two-word message into the iPhone and activated the code translator. Sure enough, the flash quickly started blinking out the message. I placed the phone on a rock at the edge of the cave so that it would be in the open and able to transmit. Then I sat next to Marilee in the mouth of the cave and put my hands in my jacket pockets. The flash kept sending my two words over and over again for all the heavens to see. I imagined them leaving the cave and going up, up, up into the dark skies overhead, traveling forever and ever…unless someone was there to receive them.

Two little words from Earth:

WE REMEMBER!

WE REMEMBER!

WE REMEMBER!

WE REMEMBER!

WE REMEMBER!

WE REMEMBER!

WE REMEMBER!

WE REMEMBER!

WE REMEMBER!

WE REMEMBER!

WE REMEMBER!

WE REMEMBER!

WE REMEMBER!

WE REMEMBER!

WE REMEMBER!

WE REMEMBER!

WE REMEMBER!

WE REMEMBER!

WE REMEMBER!

WE REMEMBER!

WE REMEMBER!

WE REMEMBER!

21
A Smelly Encounter

How do you fall asleep sitting in a cave with an iPhone flashing next to you? If it's almost midnight and you didn't sleep much the night before, I guess it's pretty easy. But before we fell asleep, we shared some more secrets, which is what best friends are really for. I told Marilee that I still liked Billy Ferguson, even if he didn't try to rescue us that night at the picnic table.

"After all," I said, "it's not like we're related. Johnny is my brother." And then Marilee shared a secret with me that almost made me go rolling down the mountain. I just couldn't believe it! I had never suspected, not in my life.

Marilee had said, "Guess who I like, Robbie." And I guessed every cute singer I could think of. Each time she said no. So I started going through the boys in our class. Davy. Noah. Evan. Nicholas. Robert. Billy. Kirk. Julian.

Oliver. Justin. Michael. Logan. James. On and on I went, and yet she said no to each name. I was about to jump up a grade until we had this conversation:

"I like Johnny."

"Johnny who?"

"Johnny McKinnon."

"Johnny McKinnon who?"

"Your brother, Johnny."

"Hold me from rolling off this mountain, Marilee."

That's what I told her and it's how I felt. My own brother! Johnny McKinnon. I never once suspected, even when she kept drooling over how brave he was. Or when she said good-bye to him in our video clip. This was going to change things big-time since I'd been known to say some nasty things about my brother. But other things had changed too. Johnny and I had grown closer since our close call.

So Marilee and I had shared our hearts with each other, and then we had both fallen asleep. I was dreaming of swimming in the river when something hairy brushed against my hand. I stirred in my dreams. "Maxwell" is what I was thinking. I reached out my hand, still asleep, and sure enough, it felt like Max's soft fur. I petted it a couple times down its back. This was when my brain started waking me up.

"You are not in bed at your house, stupid," my brain whispered. "You are in Peterson's Cave on Peterson's Mountain." I opened my eyes and sat straight up. The flash was still flickering, my message still going off into outer space. Where was the cat I was just petting? I reached down for the flashlight. Ever so quietly, I snapped it on. I saw that Marilee was sound asleep beside me, her head resting on her folded arms. Slowly, I shone the light around the cave. Nothing. Nothing. Nothing. Nothing. Skunk.

Skunk?

I had been petting a skunk in my sleep? I watched with my breath trapped in my throat as it found the half sandwich I couldn't finish before I fell asleep. It sniffed the bread all over, as if deciding whether it would taste good or not. And then its small jaws clamped down on the food and it was gone. I shook Marilee.

"Wake up," I said. "You won't believe the close encounter we just had." Not even the garbage truck would have abducted us if we'd been sprayed. Marilee sat up and rubbed her eyes.

"Are we on Mars yet?" she asked. I told her how I'd just made friends with a wild skunk.

"You weren't sprayed?"

"If I had been, you wouldn't be sitting this close to me," I told her. It's hard to believe, but a skunk smells a lot worse than bug repellent.

"Well, at least it's in the cat family," said Marilee.

I looked down over the Allagash Valley and was amazed at how it glittered in the light of the full moon. Postcard beautiful is what Grandpa always called it. Marilee shone the flashlight on her watch.

"It's almost midnight, Robbie," she said. "We really should go."

I stretched and yawned. I thought of my nice warm bed with its fat pillows and a cat curled on the end, instead of a skunk. She was right. We *should* go. But when did Roberta Angela McKinnon ever do what she should? The answer is not very often.

"Marilee, use some logic," I said. "Aliens don't know it's almost midnight on Earth. If we want them to get our message, we have to give our plan time to work."

"*Your* plan," said Marilee. But she yawned and then

rolled onto her side in her sleeping bag. I took that as a good sign. When we're on our river rocks and Marilee rolls onto her side, she's asleep in two minutes.

"Otherwise," I continued, "we're going to see Henry Helmsby's face peering out of *Fiddlehead Focus*, holding the trophy for Science Fair."

"There are worse things," Marilee said, her voice trailing off.

"Name one," I said.

Her answer was a soft little snore.

I sat huddled with my back against the cave wall. I pulled my sleeping bag tighter about me. I could hear the wind shuffling through the trees below the cave. And the sound of a logging truck shifting gears down on the highway. Some of the men who cut logs for the P. G. Irvine Company start their day at midnight. I thought of Billy Ferguson asleep in his warm bed as I wriggled my toes inside the heavy socks I was wearing. Maybe a prayer wouldn't hurt.

"Now I lay me down to sleep," I whispered, so as not to wake Marilee. Only I wasn't lying down. I was sitting up. I yawned again and this time my eyelids felt as if someone had put rocks on them. I closed my eyes, thinking of how amazed Henry Helmsby would be when a blond girl and her best friend, Marilyn or Millicent, beat him to the finish line.

* * *

It was probably a rock that rolled down the mountainside and bounced hard on the roof of the cave. Some noise, like a *bang!* woke me up. Marilee woke up too and grabbed the flashlight.

"Did you hear that?" she asked. I did. She shone the light around the cave. Nothing. Not even a caterpillar, much less a skunk. "I've had enough excitement for one night, Robbie. I'm going home."

My feet were cold and my back hurt from sleeping sitting up. Home sounded pretty darn good right then. I looked at my watch.

"It's almost one o'clock," I said. "I guess aliens don't care to meet us." I turned off the iPhone and slipped it into my jacket pocket. Marilee had picked up the sack we brought our food in and put it in my backpack.

"Well, I wasn't all that crazy about meeting *them*," she said. "Having *you* as a friend is excitement enough."

I smiled as I grabbed the handlebars and backed my bike out of the cave.

"Friend?" I asked. "We're practically sisters." Marilee punched my arm, and it wasn't a fake punch.

"You tell anyone what I said about Johnny and I swear I'll run away forever."

"I won't tell," I said. "You know I won't. Let's go home."

Headlights on, we walked our bikes down from Peterson's Cave. Riding was a little too dangerous, even with all that moonlight to guide us. The last thing I wanted to do was flatten a skunk.

"I'm going to sleep for a year," said Marilee when we reached the foot of the mountain.

"Don't worry," I told her. "I'll think of another way for us to win the science fair. But we're back to regional."

We got on our bikes and pedaled slowly along the recreational trail. Next, we would have the meadow to cross, its clover and daisies and buttercups all asleep for the night. Sometimes, I was thinking, we're lucky to live in such a safe place. It's so beautiful, come autumn, when the mosquitoes and blackflies pack up and head for Florida. Boring, maybe. But safe, and safe is not bad.

"Watch out for the big rock," Marilee said, before I could warn her of the same thing. It had been at the edge of the meadow for as long as I could remember. Dad says someone must have farmed that field once and used a team of oxen or horses to pull that big rock out of the earth. We both veered our bikes around the rock.

When we hit the meadow path, it was just safe, flat field ahead of us. Marilee pulled up alongside of me and we pedaled in unison. Side by side. Best friends for life. And that's when something seemed weird. My legs felt like they were going around and around, my feet pedaling. But I didn't seem to be moving. Was I dreaming again? Was a skunk riding the bike next to me?

"What the heck is going on?" I heard Marilee ask. I looked over. She was outlined in moonlight. I saw that her legs were also pedaling but she wasn't moving. We were making no headway at all. It was like being frozen. And yet, we didn't fall over. Our bikes stayed steady and sure.

"Marilee, what's happening?" I was afraid. I was gone

from that scary mountain and now so close to my safe home, and yet I was terrified.

"I'm not moving!" I heard her say. "I can't get my bike to move."

"Stop pedaling!" I shouted to her. "Let's try to get off these things."

"Robbie?" Her voice sounded on the verge of tears. I knew her bottom lip was trembling. I'd seen it do that so many times. "Robbie, *look up!*"

22
THE SECOND
ALLAGASH ABDUCTIONS

I did as Marilee asked, much as I hated to. I looked up, far up into the sky over our heads. Both of us sat on our bikes then, not bothering to pedal and yet not falling over. I thought I saw just stars at first, a heaven of white stars hovering over us. But then I could see the shape of the ship, triangular, twice the size of a football field, as Sheriff Mallory had described it.

"Marilee?"

"Robbie!"

Suddenly, a wide beam of light shot down from the ship's belly, lighting us up for the whole world to see, if anyone was awake and watching. But I knew better than that. It was midnight in Allagash, Maine. Five hours north of Stephen King. In the middle of the Allagash wilderness. But there we were, as lit up as Paul Ellory's red tractor and his cows and his two silos.

"We *don't* remember!" I shouted up toward the light.

"ROBBIE!"

Our legs had lifted from our bikes and we were being pulled up toward the craft. It had to be three hundred feet above the ground, just as Sheriff Mallory thought when he saw it hover over the dairy farm.

"This is too high," I thought. "We have no parachutes. What if it drops us?" My long hair had risen with the wind that engulfed us, as if it were floating on water all around my head.

"ROBBIE!" *Oh, Marilee, why do you let me talk you into such crazy stunts? My best friend. I wish you were safe at home right now.*

A hatch slid open then, right where the beam was coming from. A large door was opening into the ship. Oh no, we're really being taken! Did this happen before? How can I get away from here without breaking my neck? I looked down and saw two tiny bikes lying in the meadow, just past the big rock. One was a Schwinn Girl's Ranger, a pretty light blue, the bike Mom and Dad got me for my birthday. The other was a purple Pacific Exploit mountain bike. It once belonged to a girl named Marilee Evans. No one would ever know what happened to us.

"I want to go home!" I shouted. But my words were lost in the night winds.

Home. I could imagine it. My safe house. My safe bedroom. My wonderful family. I could almost smell the cool air up on Frog Hill just before the sun sets. I thought of four-wheeling across the meadow when the buttercups and clover are in bloom. An ice cream at Cramer's Gas & Movie Rentals. School this autumn. My cat, Maxwell. My aquarium of fish. Billy Ferguson. How could I have been bored? How could I have taken all that for granted? I was so lucky. I'd be a new person just as soon as I got home.

The beam of light had now pulled us just beneath the belly of the ship. Marilee's face turned toward me then and I saw the fear in her eyes. Her hair was also floating about her head. It would have been beautiful if we were swimming underwater near our river rocks. I could hear a whirring sound.

"You're right, Grandma," I thought. "It *is* a whirring sound."

And then we were sucked up into the spacecraft. I heard the huge door slide, and then clamp shut beneath us. Marilee was grasping my hand so hard it would hurt if I could feel it. But I was too scared to feel anything. The room we were in was filled with gray mist, like the early fog that covers the Allagash River before the sun rises. I heard a loud *whooshing* noise and the mist began to disappear. As we watched, it was sucked into openings in the floor until it was all gone. That's when I saw a silver band that encircled the entire room. It had strange writing on it, symbols and scratches and dots. I remembered that writing!

"Marilee, we've been here before!" I told her. "The four of us, that night on Peterson's Mountain, this is where they brought us!"

"How do you know that, Robbie?"

"I don't know how I know," I said. "But it all seems familiar." I stared down at Marilee's hand in mine and it was bone white.

"They should put us back, Robbie," she said. I thought I actually heard her teeth chattering. "Why would they want two stupid kids?"

"But we're not stupid, remember? We're really smart."

"If we were really smart," said Marilee, "we'd be in bed right now."

My heart beating beneath my jacket, I told myself not to panic. Surely they wouldn't hurt us. Marilee was right. We were stupid to use that Morse code on the iPhone. Okay, *I* was stupid. But sometimes even smart people do stupid things. Suddenly, we felt a change in the craft, as if its engines were revving. A charged current of energy shot through the air and circled the room.

I said nothing to Marilee, but I figured a UFO doesn't hover over a meadow so that a whole lot of people can come and gawk up at it. It would most likely zoom somewhere out of sight, just like the white balls of light we'd seen on Peterson's Mountain, zipping around the Milky Way.

"Oh my gosh," Marilee said. Her voice was trembling, and I saw tears in her eyes. "What's happening?"

"We're getting ready to take off," I said, and I did my best to sound brave. But I wasn't brave at all. My legs had turned all rubbery and it sounded like my own teeth were chattering.

"Look!" Marilee whispered. She pointed to a round

violet light that had started blinking on and off at the very top of the room. It made an eerie humming sound.

"That's the light that made us not afraid," I said. "The blue light is the one that makes us forget everything before it sends us home." But how did I know that?

Now the violet light swiveled around and stopped. It made a loud clicking sound, and then its beam shot down fast and covered Marilee and me in pale lavender light. It was so warm and soft, like a baby's blanket, that I felt the panic leaving me. And then a warm bolt of something like electricity surged through me. It was as if a halo had surrounded my entire body. And guess what? I was no longer afraid! I felt nothing but curiosity. Marilee let go of my hand and looked at me.

"I don't feel afraid at all," she said.

"Me neither," I told her. "We are definitely going to win the biggest science fair ever. We might even be given really awesome jobs at NASA."

"Robbie, if anything bad happens to me," Marilee said, "I want you to know that having you as my friend has been the best thing ever."

I felt so much love for her just then. If anything bad

was going to happen to either of us, it should happen to *me*. I deserved it and more for getting us into this. Marilee and I locked hands then. Friends for life. There was nothing else we could do. I remembered the helpless blade of hay that I'd thrown into the river current the day I talked Marilee into this crazy idea. It seemed like years ago now.

Good-bye, Mom and Dad and Johnny and Tina.

"I hope we get back home in time for my birthday," I said. "I only get to be twelve once." I thought of Mom baking me a cake and putting up silly decorations. She'd been planning my party for weeks.

"I hope I don't miss Dad's and Sarah's wedding," Marilee said. It sounded like she even meant it.

I came up with another two-word message, just like that. Lightning fast. And now, the spacecraft seemed alive with light and energy. It must have shifted into some kind of ultra-nano, super-duper-sonic speed. Probably the stuff that shoots it through wormholes.

"Get ready," Marilee whispered, her fingers wrapped tight in mine.

And that's when I shouted the two words so loud that I hoped everyone in Allagash, Maine, could hear me:

Good-bye, Earth
Good-bye, Earth
Good-bye, Earth
Good-bye, Earth
Good-bye, Earth
Good-bye, Earth
Good-bye, Earth
Good-bye, Earth
Good-bye, Earth
Good-bye, Earth
Good-bye, Earth
Good-bye, Earth
Good-bye, Earth
Good-bye, Earth
Good-bye, Earth
Good-bye, Earth
Good-bye, Earth
Good-bye, Earth
Good-bye, Earth
Good-bye, Earth
Good-bye, Earth

23
THE SPACECRAFT

As quickly as the buzz of energy had filled the ship, it disappeared. The room was spookily silent. Marilee and I let go of each other's hands. We waited, wondering what would happen next. It was good to not be afraid, that's one thing for sure.

"I don't think we moved at all," I said. It was true. All that buzzing and humming, and then nothing? Grandpa calls that "grandstanding."

"Those are windows!" Marilee was pointing at dark, narrow slits that circled the room.

"Maybe we can signal someone," I said. "Sheriff Mallory will be doing his nightly patrol. We can let him know where we are on the ship."

Marilee ran over to the closest window and peered out. I heard her gasp.

"I don't think Sheriff Mallory will see us, Robbie," she said. "Come here this second!"

I hurried over to the narrow window next to hers. I knew then what she was talking about. In the distance was a round ball I'd seen on TV many times, thanks to photographs from NASA. I could still make out the boundaries for North America and South America. Seeing it like that, so small, like a pendant on a heavenly necklace, I wondered why people fight wars when that tiny planet is our home.

"Wow," I said. "No one will ever believe this, Marilee. Ever." I'd never been that far from home before, not even when Mom and Dad took Johnny and me to Prince Edward Island to visit Anne of Green Gables.

"What if your mom went to check on us and knows now that we're missing?" Marilee said. "We should be home."

"But we're *here*, Marilee, on this awesome spaceship," I said. "We're above the Earth now, like astronauts."

"It wasn't so awesome until that violet light hit us," she reminded me. This was true. I secretly hoped the violet light didn't wear off, like Tylenol or a flu shot.

"What's that big box?" Marilee asked then. She nodded

to a large silver box that sat in one corner of the room. It was big and square, like the freezer where Grandma puts all that stuff from her garden. My mind flashed with memory. I had seen that box before. I knew I had! There was no handle on it, so I put my hand on the front and suddenly it lit up, all white and glowing. A door slid open so fast that it startled me. Before either of us could speak, metallic stairs unfolded and dropped down. I saw nothing but pale light coming from the room above.

"I guess that means we should go up those stairs," I said. "Maybe that's where the aliens are. You know, like the bridge on the *Enterprise* where Captain Kirk sits in his chair."

"Why do you think they want *us*?" Marilee asked. "I mean, I can understand if they took Henry Helmsby. He's brainy enough to be a conversation piece on another planet. The shape of his head alone would keep aliens talking for eons. But we're just two girls who get all As and prefer to live on Earth and ride our bikes."

"I think they want to find out how much we remember about the night on Peterson's Mountain," I replied. "We did send them that 'We Remember' message."

"Why would they even *care* if we remember? I mean, it's not like we can file a citizen's arrest against them. They could be light years away and we'd be eating their star-dust."

"Maybe they're really kind, you know, and don't want us earthlings to panic. They want to leave us as they found us." I remembered that Grandpa once told me that's how we should leave baby robins in their nest. "Think of the future, Marilee Evans. And get ready to be famous."

I reached for Marilee's hand and together we took the bottom step. But before we could climb, the stairs started moving, taking us up, up, up like an escalator. When it stopped, I realized that we must be at the very top of the spaceship. The room up there was dome-like and much smaller. The ceiling was covered with tiny white lights. They flickered like the fireflies back at Frog Pond. I saw a large black window on the wall. No, it wasn't a window. It was like a computer screen of some kind. Marilee and I stared up at it. It had a lot of strange writing at the sides, like hieroglyphics. On the screen was a 3-D picture of what looked like millions of stars. They were in a spiral, like the Milky Way galaxy.

"They probably came from right here in our own galaxy," I said. "There are so many stars out there, Marilee. Some of them must have planets and life-forms."

"Oh please, this isn't science class," Marilee said. "I don't care where they come from. We need to find a way off this spaceship, Robbie. This is getting too weird, violet light or not."

"Do you have any ideas *how*?" I asked.

"No, I don't. But *you* got us on here. So *you* figure it out."

I looked back at the big screen with the stars and the creepy writing. I pushed at a white button, but it didn't budge. Then I put my finger on the screen and felt a soft buzz. Now I could see through it, like a two-way window. What I saw made me pull my hand back. The stars and the writing had disappeared. In their place were dark silhouettes. I counted one, two, three, four, five heads. They'd been watching us all that time! And then, all the heads disappeared from the screen, one after the other.

"I think we're about to make some new friends," I said to Marilee.

"Violet light, don't fail me now," Marilee replied. I seconded that thought.

A door in the wall slid open and in walked a very short alien.

"Wow," I heard Marilee say, and I nodded. It, or he or she, had the most amazing eyes, which were the size and shape of hen's eggs. They weren't black at all, but the deepest and darkest blue I had ever seen. Not even Miranda Casey had eyes that blue. She stopped in front of us, those eyes peering deep. I had decided it was a female since she was a foot shorter than I am, and I'm barely five feet. She had no nose or mouth. Just those incredible eyes. They were on a head that was more round than oval. I could see occasional movements inside the head, flashes of light and color. I wondered if they were brain waves.

"Wow, wow, wow," I heard Marilee say again. I knew what she was thinking. These were definitely *not* the aliens that the Vermont Four described under hypnosis. Those aliens had smaller eyes and holes where a nose and mouth should be. But that was even better for our science project that *we* got to discover new aliens.

"Is that her skin?" I asked. "Or is she wearing a suit?"

I reached out and touched the alien's arm. It felt slippery like vinyl, like the new purse Grandma bought in Caribou. It was even the same tan color, almost like skin.

"I think it's a suit," said Marilee.

I watched as the oval eyes shimmered, as if shades were being pulled back and forth inside. It looked more like a camera shutter than a human eye. The head was a bit large for the size of her body. She had five fingers that were too long for her hands, at least in human terms. Even Mrs. Bowen, who plays piano for the church, doesn't have fingers that long. And each one had three joints. The shutters in her eyes opened and closed fast. Then I heard her thoughts. How cool was that?

"*Welcome to our ship. We will not harm you.*"

"Thank you," I said into the deep blue eyes. I nudged Marilee in her side. "Say thank you, Marilee."

"Do you thank someone for abducting you?" Marilee asked.

"*We* contacted *them*, remember?"

"Thank you for abducting us," said Marilee. The eye shutters flicked open and then closed again. This wasn't so bad. I mean, they weren't really scary ugly. Why is it that we humans always think of aliens as being a zillion times smarter than we are but really, really gross-looking?

Maybe if this alien had hair, it would be blond.

"*What do you remember?*"

"Nothing, honestly," I said. "I just have a big mouth. Ask my friend."

"She has a very big mouth," said Marilee. I shot her a look.

Now the door in the wall slid open again and five more aliens filed into the room, one behind the other. They must have been the ones whose heads I saw on the screen. There were three taller ones, what must be the males, and two more females. They were all identical. It was impossible to tell one from another. The males were taller, that's all. They paid no attention to Marilee and me. It was as if we weren't even here.

One of the males pushed the white button at the bottom of the screen. A huge instrument panel slid out of the wall. I'd never seen so many buttons and lights and round gauges. They were constantly flickering the same strange writings that I saw earlier. That must be how they pilot the spacecraft. It was like a little galaxy all its own. The three males stood in front of the panel. They each seemed to have a special job to do and their own work area. Then I saw that the joints in the fingers could work horizontally by reaching sideways.

"Look at their fingers," Marilee said. The fingers could push buttons in front of them or to the side. I tried to imagine my own fingers doing that. Maybe Mrs. Bowen could teach me to play the piano after all.

The female who came first to greet us was still staring at me, and it was making me a little uncomfortable. It reminded me of that *Twilight Zone* show that Marilee was dumb enough to mention. "To Serve Man." I hoped this alien wasn't wondering if I tasted like chicken.

"*What is your mission?*"

"Tell the truth," Marilee whispered to me. "We want to win at science fair."

"Ah, well," I said. "We're just two curious kids from Earth who want to go where no man has gone before." It was sort of the truth. I saw the dark eyes working.

"*Star Trek.*"

"Awesome," said Marilee. "They watch *Star Trek*!"

"Don't be silly," I said. "It's because all the television and radio airwaves leave Earth and travel out into space.

That's probably how they learned about us earthlings in the first place. Old TV and radio shows."

The other two females had gone to stand in front of the black screen above the flashing instrument panel. I saw them working their long fingers on the dials there. The 3-D picture of the stars kept changing. Star systems appeared and disappeared. Again, the female gave me her large oval eyes. Shutters opened and closed in those dark baby blues.

"*What are your questions?*"

"For starters," I said, "why did you abduct us the other night?"

"*We wish to study new life-forms in our galaxy.*"

"Do you collect hair and skin samples?" asked Marilee.

"*No, we study only the brain waves of you earthlings to determine how you have evolved.*"

"What constellation are you from?" I asked then. "I mean, in Earth language." This was the most amazing thing that will ever happen to me in my life, unless Billy Ferguson kisses me one day. Here I was interviewing an alien on a spaceship, and who knows how far from Earth we were right then.

"*We are from the constellation of Libra.*"

"I knew it!" said Marilee.

"Gliese 581, the red dwarf star in Libra," I said. "It has planets orbiting it, but the one with possible life is planet g, in the habitable zone." I was showing off again, and in front of an alien with an IQ of probably 500,000, but I couldn't help myself. "Are you from planet g?" I asked. "We studied about it in school."

"*We have come from the place that you call planet g.*"

I looked at Marilee, excited.

"We aren't going to *work* at NASA," I whispered. "We're going to *own* it."

"How long did it take you to travel to Earth?" Marilee asked. I was wondering the same thing since 20.5 light years wasn't like driving to Bangor for Christmas shopping, even in a snowstorm.

"*We do not think in terms of time, as you earthlings do. For us, time does not exist.*"

I thought about this. "It exists if you've been grounded," I said. That's when I knew for sure that aliens, at least *these* aliens, had no sense of humor. The big eyes simply stared at me.

"Why don't you land at the White House?" That's one thing my Grandpa would have wanted me to ask for sure. "Or at the Super Bowl?"

"*Earthlings are not ready.*"

"Do you have a photo of yourself?" Marilee asked. "We need one for our school project."

The blue-black eyes glowed as they interpreted the question. It was as if the eyes were recording everything.

"*This will not be permitted. Do you have more questions?*" I saw the shutters working inside again.

"Well, sure," I said. "Can we have information on your planet then? Can you give us some facts? You know, in terms we can understand on Earth?"

The female turned to look at the large black screen. The shutters worked again in her enormous eyes, and then the screen filled with all kinds of facts and figures. I felt my mouth drop open.

Parent Star		
Star		Gliese 581
Constellation		Libra
Right ascension	(α)	15^h 19^m 26^s
Declination	(δ)	–07° 43' 20"
Apparent magnitude	(mv)	10.55
Distance		20.3 ± 0.3 ly
		(6.2 ± 0.1 pc)
Spectral style		M3V
Mass	(m)	0.31 M
Radius	(r)	0.29 R
Temperature	(T)	3480 ± 48 K
Metallicity	[Fe/H]	–0.33 ± 0.12
Age		7 – 11 Gyr
Orbital Elements		
Semimajor Axis	(a)	0.14601 ±
		0.00014 AU
Eccentricity	(e)	0
Orbital period	(P)	36.562 ± 0.052 d
		(0.100 y)
		(877 h)
Mean anomaly	(M)	271 ± 48
Semi-amplitude	(K)	1.29 ± 0.19m/s

"Someone is showing off," I whispered to Marilee. "And this time it's not me."

"Where did you get all these facts?" Marilee asked.

The alien turned to look at her. The shutters shimmered again as the eyes opened and closed.

"*Wikipedia.*"

Marilee and I sighed together in our disappointment.

"We need facts that other earthlings still don't know," I explained. "We want to be *the first* to discover something."

And then an odd thing happened. I saw one of the other females stop the work she was doing at the instrument panel. She stood behind the female next to her and pushed a finger against her back. A door popped open. I saw all kinds of intricate stuff. She was pushing buttons on a panel inside, like programming a computer. And that's when I got it.

"Marilee," I said, "they're not real. They're machines."

"Are you sure?" Marilee asked. "The eyes look amazing. Why would they be robots?"

"Because, think about it," I said. It made total sense to me. I remembered seeing a TV program about it. "Life on that planet is so intelligent they would have created machines to do the travel for them. Top-of-the-line hardware. Artificial intelligence. Our scientists are trying to create it on Earth even now. But we're hundreds of years away from doing it like this."

That explained the camera action in the eyes. And then I realized that there was no male and no female! They were just intelligent machines with specific jobs to perform. On their planet, the idea of an old-fashioned spongy brain doing all the thinking had probably been out of date for a ca-zillion years.

Then the machine standing in front of us tilted its head forward. The shutters in its eyes moved rapidly, as if it was receiving information from somewhere. I watched as the shimmering eyes expanded and contracted, like the pupil in a human eye. I reached out and touched the surface. It was hard, made of something like glass or plastic. Marilee touched the face.

"It's a kind of material," she said. "You're right. This is a machine."

"It's being controlled, probably by life-forms back on planet g," I said.

"I wonder if they look like this," said Marilee.

"I think they made them like this so that we earthlings won't die ten thousand deaths when we see one."

"So we just die *one* death?" Marilee asked. "It has no mouth or nose, Robbie!"

"There are a hundred billion galaxies out there, Marilee," I said. "So there are that many different ways the aliens on planet g might look."

The machine was now done receiving information. Its head tilted back, and the egg-shaped eyes looked right at *me*.

"*Please give me the apparatus.*"

"Excuse me?"

"*Please give me the apparatus.*" The right arm lifted up and the hand spun around to show a flat palm. The hand was waiting for me.

"What does it want from you?" Marilee asked.

Okay, it was true that I still had Mom's iPhone in my jacket pocket. I had hoped no one would notice. It was my last chance to snap a photo of the inside of the spaceship.

"*Please give me the apparatus.*"

"You are such a spoilsport," I said. But I took the

phone out of my pocket and plunked it down on the upturned hand. It immediately pulled back and spun around and flicked on the iPhone. Wow, it happened so fast. As I watched, the head tilted forward so that the eyes could focus on the phone. The shutters were working fast inside. I saw the phone's camera screen flash brightly. Then I was handed back the "apparatus."

"Thanks," I said. "Now, about that picture I'd like to take…"

But before I could finish, the alien machine reached out and touched a finger against my forehead, right between my eyes. I felt a kind of *zap*!

"That was weird," I said. It felt like an ice cube was held against my skin.

"Please let us take a picture," Marilee begged. "How else can we win even a regional science fair?"

"Have you ever abducted Henry Helmsby?" I asked. "If you had, you'd know why this is so important to us." If they didn't help, this UFO-chasing had been a lot of work for nothing. I could have learned yoga. Helped Mom paint the garage. Started an ant farm.

"*You must trust yourself.*"

Okay, suddenly this machine was Oprah? But before I could protest anymore, I heard a clicking. Even before I looked up, I knew what it was. The blue light. The one that would make us forget. I remembered it from that night on Peterson's Mountain. It was also the light that would send us home. Well, I guess that's better than becoming a human slave on planet g. Then the light hit us and I could see Marilee's face in a bluish glow. In an instant, we were in the room we first came to, the one filled with gray mist that reminded me of early fog on the Allagash River.

"Wow," Marilee said. "How did that happen?"

"I don't know," I admitted. "But I guess they would know how to teleport." It made sense that they could send matter from one place to another without having to drive it there in Dad's pickup truck. We were way behind on Earth.

"What's that?" Marilee asked, and I saw a second blue light beaming overhead. I knew why. Just before I couldn't remember anything, I felt a deep pride that it would take *two* blue lights to make Roberta Angela McKinnon forget.

"*Trust yourself.*"

And then everything went blank.

24
THE RETURN

"We do not think in terms of time, as you earthlings do. For us, time does not exist."

Watch out for the big rock," Marilee said before I could warn her of the same thing. It had been at the edge of the meadow for as long as I could remember. We were on our way back from Peterson's Cave, having failed at contacting aliens. We both veered our bikes around the rock. When we hit the meadow path, it was just safe, flat field ahead of us. Stars twinkled like fireflies over our heads. Marilee pulled up alongside of me and we pedaled in unison, side by side.

"I had the strangest dream tonight, Marilee," I told her.

"Yes, you dreamed that you were petting Max when you were petting a skunk," she said and laughed at the idea.

"No, I dreamed another one after that," I said. "It must have been the second time I fell asleep. I just can't seem to remember much of it." It was true. I had bits and pieces of memory. Flashes, like fireflies. I remembered eyes, so big and round and blue. And didn't we talk to creatures with funny-looking fingers? "I think in the dream we were abducted by aliens from the planet g."

"Well, no wonder," said Marilee. "It's all we've been talking about for weeks!"

"I guess you're right," I said.

"Don't be disappointed that your plan didn't work," Marilee said. "It was still fun."

"Maybe we should try again tomorrow," I suggested. "Maybe the aliens were just too busy tonight to abduct us." It was possible. Maybe it was movie night on the spacecraft.

"Don't worry," Marilee said. "I'm sure you'll come up with another crazy plan for the science fair. Something better than the hollydock."

I had already thought about this. We had several options, as I saw it. If those didn't work, I was destined to lose to Henry Helmsby again. But at least this year I had a partner. That meant it would hurt half as much.

"I have five ideas in mind," I said.

"Five?" Even knowing me as she does, Marilee was surprised.

"First off, there's Allagash Lake," I said. "The Indian tribes who were here first told stories of a creature that lives in the murky waters at the bottom. You know, like the Loch Ness monster over in Scotland. Grandma grew up on the lake and she saw it once. She said it looked like a fifty-foot inchworm."

I heard Marilee's bike chain creak, as if maybe she was pedaling a bit faster.

"If I had a choice in the matter, and I rarely do," she said, "I'd pass on that one."

"Then, look at where we live, Marilee," I said. "Those two hunters who claim they saw Bigfoot at the abandoned logging camps were pretty believable. One is a doctor and one is a professor. Uncle Horace said if they'd been a lawyer and a politician he wouldn't believe a word of it. But he knows Dr. Blanchard personally. If Uncle Horace believes it, it's worth considering."

"I'm not exactly dying to meet Bigfoot," said Marilee, and her pedaling picked up the pace again.

"Well, there are gold coins from the Revolutionary War buried somewhere in Peterson's Cave," I said. "Folks around here claim that Old Man Peterson said so with his dying words a hundred years ago. The coins belonged to his great-grandfather. Everyone looked, and then everyone gave up. I bet Calley's ghost knows where the coins are. I bet she'd tell us if we held a séance up there. Is gold safe enough for you, O Gutless Girl?"

When Marilee didn't answer, I smiled. I knew I was making her very nervous. I'm good at doing that. It's just a talent I have. We rolled past the sleeping buttercups and nodding clover, and were almost to Frog Pond when Marilee said, "Maybe we should learn to shop until we drop, like some of the girls in our class. It would be a lot less scary."

I couldn't see us at the mall, trying on hats and smelling perfume samples. You want to see scary? It's Marilee and me in designer dresses with matching purses.

"And then, everyone knows that the old Baker mansion is haunted," I continued. "We can install Ghost Radar on

Mom's iPhone. I could even download the application tomorrow. Are you ready to interview a ghost?"

"Not really."

"Then what about what Mr. Finley says? That a werewolf runs with a pack of wild timber wolves across the river in Quebec. The French call it the *loup-garou*."

"Please," said Marilee. "Werewolves don't scare me. They look like shaggy dogs with bad teeth."

"We have five adventures to choose from," I said. "As Grandpa always said, the world is our oyster."

"What does that *mean*?" asked Marilee.

"I have no idea," I said. "There's no seafood in northern Maine."

And that's when something seemed weird. The path in front of us was suddenly lit up with bright light.

"*Help!*" I shouted to Marilee. "We're being abducted!" So much for my dazzling courage.

Marilee braked and I did the same. That's when I saw that the lights came from behind us, two yellow headlights, like buttercup eyes in the night. It was a car and not a spaceship! Sheriff Mallory stopped his patrol car and got out.

"I knew I saw bikers riding down the mountainside," he said. "But I never dreamed it was you two girls. Do you realize it's two o'clock in the morning?" The sound of his door closing echoed back from Frog Pond. "Do your parents know where you are?"

I straddled my bike and waited until he was standing next to me.

"Do you want me to lie or tell the truth?" I asked. "I'm prepared to do either."

Sheriff Mallory smiled. As I said, he thinks I'm a little adult. A real cut-up, is what he told my dad.

"Never mind then," he said. "Just get yourselves home before anything wild happens. I'll be glad when the full moon is over."

"Did you find Joey Wallace?" Marilee asked.

"He found himself," said the sheriff. "He turned up at his mother's door, all bug-eyed and hungry. He says he ran out of gas, so he pulled his jeep off to the side of the road and called his girlfriend to come get him."

"Wow," I said. "I never knew Joey could go that long without his favorite fishing hat."

"He didn't even know he'd dropped it," Sheriff Mallory

continued. "He said he intended to buy a few gallons of gas and come back for the jeep. But then his girlfriend reminded him that World Wrestling Entertainment was having a marathon weekend on TV. Joey didn't want to miss a single headlock, hammerlock, kick, or punch. So he went home with her to Caribou and forgot all about his jeep."

"You mean he pulled a joke this time without even meaning to?" asked Marilee.

"Yup," said Sheriff Mallory, nodding. "His mother is some kind of angry about it too."

"The boy who cried werewolf," I said, "even when he didn't mean to."

"What were you doing on Peterson's Mountain this time of night?" asked Sheriff Mallory.

"We were trying to contact a UFO," I admitted. "Like the one you saw."

"You *did* see a UFO, didn't you?" Marilee asked.

"Well, girls, I suppose I did," said the sheriff. "But one thing is for sure. If there are aliens out there, they'll contact us when *they* think the time is right. Not when *we* think it is. I've learned something these past weeks. There are times when we just have to live without logical explanations."

"I guess so," I said. An image flashed just then in my mind. I saw a big computer screen filled with all kinds of stars and strange writing. Did I dream about a spaceship and an alien with large egg-shaped eyes? My brain was working hard to remember.

"You girls be careful riding home now," Sheriff Mallory said.

We told him thanks a lot for remembering what it's like to be a kid. Then we watched his headlights disappear across the meadow.

"Wait a second, Marilee," I said. "What time did the sheriff say it was? Did I hear correctly?"

"You're right," said Marilee. "He said it was two a.m. But that's not possible. It wasn't even one o'clock yet when we left the cave."

I held my wrist in front of the headlight on my bike and saw Marilee do the same to hers.

"It's two o'clock," Marilee said. "But how can that be, Robbie?"

I shook my head. I didn't know. It was really weird.

"The only thing I can figure out," I said, "is that I was wrong when I checked my watch. We must have slept longer than we thought."

We set off again on our bikes, and that's when it happened. I felt a cold round spot right in the middle of my forehead. It was like someone was holding an ice cube there.

"*Stop!*" I shouted to Marilee. We both braked and sat on our bikes.

"What's wrong, Robbie?"

"I don't know," I said. "This funny feeling just came over me." I reached into my pocket, for no logical reason, and pulled out Mom's iPhone. I mean, there's no reception in Allagash, so why was I doing that? I turned it on and then, with Marilee watching, I pushed the record button for the phone's camera. It seemed like a voice in my head told me to point the screen toward the constellation Libra, which was still quite high in the sky. Voice or no voice, it's natural I'd pick Libra since that's the sign I was born under, on October 15. But why was I trying to record a constellation so late at night from Earth? I don't know. I guess it's the wild gene.

"What are you doing?" Marilee asked. She got off her bike and put the kickstand down.

"I'm not sure," I said. The cold spot between my eyes was tingling now. I hoped I wasn't coming down with the flu or something worse. I'd like to go my whole life without knowing what it's like to get chicken pox. And that's when a small, round light appeared on the phone's screen and just stayed there. I held the phone steady in my hand, still pointing at the stars in Libra. Almost four minutes passed before the light finally disappeared. I felt my breath catch in my throat.

"Marilee," I said. "Start thinking International Science Fair again."

"What do you mean?" Marilee was staring up into the sky. "I don't see anything unusual."

"Not with the naked eye you don't," I said. "But the phone's LCD screen just picked up a flash from Libra. It can detect infrared light, even if our eyes can't. Do you know what this means?"

"I think so," said Marilee. "But it's too awesome to even imagine."

"If you think it's awesome, then you're thinking right,"

I said. "That infrared flash is the shock wave that a star sends out before it collapses." I paused, almost too excited to hear the words I planned to say next. "Marilee, there's a star in Libra that's about to go supernova. And we're probably the only human beings on earth who know it."

As soon as I said those words, the cold spot on my forehead disappeared. Far off on the horizon, I saw a round white light, too big and bright to be a star or a planet.

"Look!" Marilee said, and pointed. As we watched, the bright light zoomed across the sky in a nanosecond. It stopped directly overhead, a shiny round pearl. That piece of memory jumped back into my mind just then. Big, blue egg-shaped eyes. Then, before we could even blink, the ball of light simply disappeared.

"That's a spaceship," I said to Marilee. "It's not a UFO. It's a spaceship from the planet g." I had no idea what made me say that. But I felt it was true, somehow.

"It's your dream again," said Marilee. "But girl-friend, who cares about UFOs when we're about to *predict* a supernova? That's only happened one time before. Four Hs hasn't got a chance with his stupid hollydock." She was totally right. So I forgot about the ball of light and my bits of memory and the cold spot on my forehead.

"When I get up tomorrow," I told her, "I'll call the Southern Maine Astronomers group down in Portland. I'll tell them to monitor Libra because there's gonna be a supernova there soon. And I'll mention how McKinnon-Evans isn't a bad name to give it."

We sat on the grass of the field and stared up into the sky. Without speaking, we were trying to imagine how amazing this night had turned out to be after all. Maybe we didn't contact aliens, except in the dream I had. At least, I think it was a dream. But we would soon be two of only three people on earth to *predict* a supernova. We knew we weren't the youngest girls to *discover* one. We had been envious—okay, we were really jealous—of a Canadian girl named Kathryn Aurora Gray, who lived just down the river from us in Fredericton, New Brunswick. She was only ten years old when she discovered her first supernova. But she had computer images to guide her and help from her dad. We had Mom's iPhone and the wild gene.

"This is the most awesome night of my life," Marilee whispered.

"Mine too," I said.

"But we've peaked at age eleven, Robbie. How can it get any more exciting than this?"

"It can if we take a werewolf to the dentist," I said.

I heard Marilee giggle.

"You know I'm game, don't you?" she said.

Of course, I knew. That's why, sometimes, I wished that we could stay eleven years old forever. Before the year ended, we'd both be twelve. And then we'd have only one year left to *really* be kids. A lot of things start to change when you turn thirteen.

"You know what predicting a supernova means, don't you?" I asked, and Marilee nodded.

"We'll be way beyond famous," she said.

"Overnight," I added.

We sat for a time thinking about that. I'm not sure how Marilee saw us becoming famous. But I imagined long black limousines pulling up to my house and having a hard time finding a place to turn around in our driveway. Maybe they would knock down our back-yard fireplace in the process or run over Tina's Little Tykes Push & Ride Racer. I saw bottles of nonalcoholic champagnes and wines being poured around the clock. Shirley Temples for everyone. They might even want us to wear designer clothes, just so Vera Wang or Donna Karan could say they dressed us. I mean, the second people ever in the whole history of the world to predict a supernova were two kids from northern Maine? And one of them is a natural blond? This is *big*. We would have to put in a guest bedroom for Anderson Cooper. In a week's time, we'd be sick of Oprah calling us. "It's *her* again," my mom would say, sighing a big sigh as she handed me the phone. Mom always said that kids like Michael Jackson and Britney Spears had their childhoods stolen. Children should stay children for as long as they can, according to Mom, because childhood happens only once.

"What do you *really* want more than anything in the world?" I asked Marilee. "Is it to be famous?" I heard her fidgeting in her jacket pocket and then she offered me a cough drop. I shook my head and waited as she unwrapped one and plopped it into her mouth.

"Honestly," she said, "I'd like for my mom and dad to get back together again."

"But I thought you liked Sarah," I said. "I thought you welcomed her with open arms."

"My arms are open enough," said Marilee, "since she's nice and all and I have no choice in the matter. But, I mean, you only get two parents in your life, Robbie." I nodded. Life can deal some kids a crappy hand. But at least her two parents were good parents and they both loved her no end. "Sarah could marry someone else and be just as happy," Marilee added.

"Yeah, I know," I said. "But that's not going to happen, Marilee."

"I know," she said. "What do *you* want more than anything?"

I didn't have to think long about that one.

"I want Grandpa to be alive again," I said. It was truer than anything I'd said in my life. I wanted him to see me win the science fair. And afterward, he'd come up all beaming to hug me. "You're not only my favorite blond granddaughter," he'd say, "but you're my smartest." This is funny when you remember that Tina is only four years old. Maybe the biggest science project of all is learning to live without people you love.

"But that's not going to happen," said Marilee. "Your grandpa is not coming back."

I knew it. So we sat there, side by side, thinking about our lives. I knew then that we wouldn't tell anyone about the supernova, just so we could stay kids for as long as possible. But in my heart I named it the Robert "Bob" Carter supernova. That made me feel better, as if every time I looked up at Libra, I'd think of my grandpa. And when Henry Helmsby wins first place at the science fair, I'll walk right up to him and say, "Congratulations, Henry, you deserve to win." And I'll shake the claw-like hand that is attached to his crab-like arm. I won't mean a word of it, of course, but I'll "cowboy up," which is what Grandpa always told me I should do.

"Marilee," I said. "I don't want to be famous."

"Neither do I." I heard her let out a big breath.

"Let's go home," I said then.

We got on our bikes and pedaled past Frog Hill. All of the frogs were excited in Frog Pond. Maybe frogs know how to predict supernovas too. Above our heads the heaven glittered with stars. Up ahead in the distance,

I saw the yellow light I'd left on in my bedroom. Soon, Marilee and I would be safe in bed and sound asleep. I might have a big mouth sometimes, but there are other times when I keep things to myself. Such as the fact that Grandma never once dated Sheriff Mallory. She just always said that to make Grandpa jealous. "But don't tell her I know the difference, okay, Robbie?" Grandpa made me promise the day he shared that secret with me. "It keeps our marriage interesting."

Even though I know a lot of things for a country girl in the middle of a wilderness, there are some things I just don't *need* to know. For instance, I don't need to know what it's like to be abducted by aliens. Or how it might feel to ride through the Milky Way on a spaceship, even faster than we fly on our four-wheelers past Frog Pond. I don't have to think about life on other planets when there's so much fun to have on Earth.

All I need to think about is how I'll soon be twelve and Mom will throw a big party for me. My whole family will sing "Happy Birthday," and Grandma will hit high notes that will make Mr. Finley's dog howl from a quarter mile down the road. And Billy Ferguson will finally kiss me, a real fast kiss, when the two of us meet in the creepy shadows of Mom's lilac bushes.

When spring comes again, I'll run down to the poplar tree near Frog Pond and climb up to see if there are sky-blue eggs in the nest. And I'll go back later on to count the baby birds. I'll keep going back until the babies have all flown and there are just tiny feathers left to prove they were ever there.

Mr. Einstein, the genius, once said that there is no difference between the past and the future. So, I thought about *now,* about the *present.* I thought of how much fun Marilee and I will have before we grow up for good, while we're still country kids who live five hours north of Stephen King. And I thought about riding our snowmobiles next winter, flying across the snow-covered meadow, our breath just cold, gray puffs in the wintry air.

That's all I had to think about. So Marilee Evans and I pedaled home, tired and ready for bed. We pedaled our bikes across the meadow full of sleeping buttercups and nodding clover.

We pedaled side by side.

Friends for life.

Acknowledgments

Tom Viorikic, my husband, who patiently lives with each novel and is always my first reader.

My sister, **Joan St. Amant,** my first muse and constant support. And her granddaughters, **Lily St. Amant** and **Isabelle St. Amant**, my great-nieces who are soon to be middle grade readers.

My wonderful editor **Steve Geck,** with whom I have wanted to work for oh so many years. Also the fine team at Jabberwocky: my assistant editor **Cat Clyne**, production editor **Jillian Bergsma**, design lead **Will Riley**, and my publicist **Heather Moore** (and welcome to the planet Earth, **Abigail Moore!**).

Many thanks to **Dr. John Millis, PhD**, who teaches physics and astronomy at Anderson University, and who came through for me when I had an "astronomy plot problem" that I needed to solve for this story.

Thanks to those others who read early drafts, especially **Kathleen Wallace King** (who put the genre of middle grade into my mind) but also **Larry Wells, Randy Ford, Rosemary Kingsland, Rosemary Monahan, Sarah LeClaire,** and **Cheryl Carlesimo.**

Don Chouinard and daughters **Olivia Chouinard** and **Cassidy Chouinard**, for answering questions about young minds.

Emma Grace Pelletier, for her help with my "middle-grade" questions.

To those who allowed me to use their names for this novel: **Darlene Kelly Dumond** (it's really **Two Rivers Café**, and not **The River Café**); **Faye Hafford**, at the Faye O'Leary Hafford Library, here in Allagash; **Wayne McBreairty**, not "McBridy," who does not manage canoe rentals; My great-nieces **Caitlin Overlock, Shawna Cathie O'Neal,** and **Lexi Desjardins; Allagash Wood Products**, the shop owned by my brother and nephew, **Louis Pelletier, Jr.** and **Louis Pelletier III**; and **Chad Putnam**, who really does drive for UPS; brother **Vernon**

Pelletier and wife **Sylvia Martin Pelletier**, who do not own a tree farm; **Lila Jandreau**, who faithfully delivers our mail to Allagash; **Bill Flagg**, who does Community Relations for Cary Memorial Hospital and does not own a grocery store; **Sherry Sullivan**, who does not own a pink Cadillac, but probably wishes she did; **Andrew Birden**, who really is the publisher of *Fiddlehead Focus*; **Doody Michaud**, the real Chief of Police in Fort Kent, Maine; **Carl Hileman**, for "Charlie Hileman;" My old college pal **Larry "Fitz" Fitzherbert**, who is a mailman from Fort Kent, not Allagash; and **Angel Dionne** for "Mrs. Dionne." Great-nieces **Sydni Pelletier** and **Lydia Pelletier**.

And thanks to **Louis Glaser, Candyce Williams Glaser, Allen Jackson,** and **Nancy Henderson**, for their kind support. And a special mention to **Taylor Pond Evans** and to **Emma Masse**, both young cousins with the writing bug.

In memory of **Evan McBreairty** (1992–2013) for his daddy, Wayne.

Also, in memory of my great-grandfather **Nizarre Pelletier** (1836–1924) whose story is falsely told to Robbie in this book as happening to **George McKinnon**, also my great-grandfather. The real story: Nizarre first married **Mary Jane Hughes**, who died in childbirth while he was away working in the woods for the winter. He later married my great-grandmother, **Mary Jane Hafford**. Their son, **Thomas Pelletier** (1886–1986), was my grandfather. He ran the ferryboat across the Allagash River for thirty-three summers, until the bridge was built.

And here's to the evening spent in Orono, Maine with these amazing women who read an advance copy of *The Summer Experiment*. We shared a lot of food, a lot of wine, and a lot of laughter: **Laurie Carpenter, Naomi Bentivoglio, Janet Elvidge, Janice Graham, Louise Jolliffe**, and **Joyce Wiebe**.

About the Author

Cathie Pelletier was born and raised on the banks of the St. John River, at the end of the road in northern Maine. She is the author of nine other novels, including *The Funeral Makers* (NYTBR Notable Book), *The Weight of Winter* (winner of the New England Book Award), and *Running the Bulls* (winner of the Paterson Prize for Fiction). As K. C. McKinnon, she has written two novels, both of which became television films. After years of living in Nashville, Tennessee; Toronto, Canada; and Eastman, Quebec, she has returned to Allagash, Maine, and the family homestead where she was born. Her forthcoming novel, *A Year After Henry*, will be published by Sourcebooks, Inc. in summer 2014.